Murder at the Horse Show

A Midlife Paranormal Cozy Mystery Book 1

Emily Blake

Chapter One

Having to get up at 4:30 a.m. is nature's way of asking, "How committed are you REALLY to this midlife adventure?"

I wrestled into beige breeches that seemed designed to highlight every pizza-related life choice.

"Pizza was definitely a crime against future horse show self," I muttered. Stress eating: 1, Future Rider Jen: 0.

Every extra curve seemed more pronounced, and the wrinkles that had been setting up shop on my face over the last few years appeared even deeper.

How is it that I already had jowls? The reflection that stared back at me was a woman I barely recognized.

Behind me, Ripley—the world's most opinionated Boston Terrier and self-proclaimed arbiter of taste—sat on the bathmat, watching my struggle like a judge on some reality TV show. His head tilted to one side in a way that always made me wonder if he was genuinely concerned or just calculating the perfect moment to add his signature snort of judgment.

He'd been my shadow ever since the kids left for

college, his constant commentary both a comfort and a reminder that I was never alone.

Those bright eyes tracked my every awkward shimmy and hop as I tried to smooth myself out, and I swear I could feel the weight of his critique.

"What do you think?" I asked, glancing at his reflection.

He tilted his head, his big, expressive eyes narrowing slightly. His thoughts came through clear as day.

Those pants make your butt look like two loaves of bread stuffed in a grocery bag.

"Jeez, thanks for the vote of confidence." I sighed, tugging my breeches higher to hide the muffin top while tucking in my new white show shirt. The crisp cotton felt stiff and uncomfortable against my skin, tighter and less flattering than I remembered when trying it on at the tack shop.

"You know, most dogs would just be snoring under the covers at this ungodly hour. But not you and your fashion police routine."

Most dogs aren't as honest as me. He flopped onto his back, legs waving in the air as he scratched at an itch. *Someone's got to tell you the truth.*

"Right, because I needed a reminder that I'm a frumpy middle-aged woman when I'm about to go do my first horse show ever."

Just keeping it real, Treat Lady.

I looked at myself, the years etched across my face—kids growing up, the divorce, the steady march of time. Here I stood, at fifty-one years old, about to compete in my first-ever horse show against fearless kids with bows in their hair.

Mark would have shaken his head, just like he did when I said I was going to take riding lessons, calling it my "midlife crisis on horseback."

But this wasn't about him anymore. Or my kids.

It was finally about me.

"This isn't too crazy, right? Or is it?" My hands shook as I pulled sweats over my new breeches to keep them clean. The soft fabric provided a temporary refuge from my self-consciousness. "Normal people my age take up gardening."

You've never been normal, Ripley snorted, rolling back to his feet with a little grunt. *Besides, Cooper likes you.*

Cooper. The steady school horse who'd taught me more about trust in the past year than my ex-husband had in twenty. His gentle brown eyes and patient nature had given me a confidence I never knew I had.

Still, jumping fences on a thousand-pound animal at my age...

I zipped up my coat and grabbed my boot bag, helmet, and gloves, each item a reminder of the craziness I was about to embark on.

I reached into my pocket to check for Cooper's peppermints—his favorite reward for putting up with my amateur attempts at equitation. Just feeling them reminded me of the relationship we'd built together over the past year. I wouldn't have even dreamed of doing this if it weren't for him.

"Wait here, Ripley," I said, nudging him gently as he followed me toward the door. I carried everything out to the car, the crisp air biting at my cheeks. After loading the gear into the back seat, I returned inside.

"Okay, your turn. Where's your stuff?" I grabbed Ripley's water bowl, treats, and the plaid dog bed he insisted on bringing everywhere. "You've got the easy job today—looking adorable and judging me."

I've got you covered, he said, his little butt wiggling with a confidence I could only dream of as he trotted to the door.

3

I closed the door to my house and stood by the car. Everything was packed and ready, but I still felt like something was missing—maybe a stiff drink or a good excuse to back out.

∼

Gʀᴀᴠᴇʟ ᴄʀᴜɴᴄʜᴇᴅ under the truck's tires as Liz navigated into Pine Valley's crowded parking area. My stomach lurched with each bump. The parking lot was a sea of trucks and trailers—from gleaming rigs that probably cost more than my house to weathered veterans showing every mile of their journey.

I could relate.

Liz had convinced me this was the perfect show to get my feet wet—low pressure, a mix of beginners and seasoned riders, and no long hauls. She'd made it sound so reasonable, like dipping my toes into a calm, shallow pool.

Now that I was here, it felt more like getting shoved off a dock.

"Deep breaths," Liz said as she maneuvered the truck and trailer. "You've practiced for this."

Was I being that obvious? I gave her what I hoped would be a smile and put on my game face, though it probably looked more like a grimace.

Liz laughed. Yep, grimace it was.

The truck eased to a stop near the stalls, the trailer settling behind us as Liz cut the engine. My legs were shaky as I climbed down from the cab. Ripley practically vibrated with excitement as he jumped out alongside me.

His head darted back and forth as he took in the noise and activity. *This place smells like hay and overpriced carrots*, he said, eyes wide.

"Come on," I murmured under my breath, hoping Liz wouldn't notice me conversing with my Boston Terrier. "Try to blend in."

Blend in? Are you kidding? Everyone loves me. I don't blend in anywhere, Ripley quipped, trotting ahead like he owned the place.

Amy, my barn buddy and go-to source for equestrian advice aside from Liz, pulled into a spot nearby with her bay mare Belle in tow. She hopped out of her truck with the practiced calm of someone who'd been navigating horse shows for decades, coffee cup in hand.

"Morning!" she called with a grin, heading toward us. "Ready for some horse show chaos? This is going to be so much fun!"

Her confidence was contagious—or at least I hoped it would be. I gave her a half-hearted wave, trying to match her energy, but my stomach still felt like it was hosting a gymnastics meet.

A small crowd of Liz's other students arrived, converging on the trailer, each person knowing exactly what to do. I hung back, watching them untie lead ropes and lower the ramp with the kind of efficiency that made me feel even more like a rookie.

When it was Cooper's turn, Liz motioned for me to go in the trailer to get him. I had no idea what I was doing, but I passed off Ripley to Amy and went in. Cooper backed out like a pro, not needing my help in the least aside from ensuring he didn't step on his lead rope. Once out, he took in his surroundings with the calm interest of a horse who'd seen it all.

His thoughts drifted into my mind. *Ah, show day. Time to make you look good while I do all the work.*

"Very funny," I said quietly, drawing comfort from his

solid presence. Cooper's warmth radiated through my hands as I stroked his neck, his nearly white coat gleaming in the morning sun.

I can feel it. Your stomach is a mess, and you're over-thinking, as usual. He nudged my pocket where the pepper-mints lived, his velvet nose expertly finding the exact spot. *It's just another day of jumping over sticks. We've done this at home plenty of times.*

His matter-of-fact tone made me smile despite my nerves. Trust Cooper to reduce first horse show nerves to something as simple as "jumping over sticks."

Yes, but normally there's no one watching me besides Liz, I replied silently.

Judges are just humans who think they know better than everyone. They're not always right, you know. Especially in the hunters. But they love me. Now, about those pepper-mints... I know you've got some...

Behind us, Ripley strained at his leash in Amy's grip, his entire body wiggling with excitement. *This place is amazing! So many horses! So many people! So many things to sniff!*

"Well, one of us is having a blast already," I joked, gesturing toward the quivering ball of energy disguised as a Boston Terrier.

"He's not the only one who should be excited. Remember, this is supposed to be fun," Amy said, flashing me a smile. She motioned in the direction of the stalls. "Come on, let's get Cooper and Belle settled and then go watch some rounds. Nothing cures show nerves like realizing everyone else is just as frazzled as you are while pretending they're fine."

ONCE BELLE and Cooper were happily settled in their stalls with fresh shavings, water, and hay, Amy, Ripley, and I wandered over to the hunter warm-up ring. The morning sun cast long shadows across the arena as riders worked their horses. Hooves thudded softly against the sandy footing, sending up faint puffs of dust.

"If you can't count your strides properly, you don't belong here!" a voice sliced through the ambient chatter like a whip crack.

The voice belonged to a woman who stood near the center of the warm-up ring, her arms crossed tightly over her chest, sharp eyes following a horse and rider. Even from this distance, I could make out her commanding presence—tall and straight-backed, with silver hair pulled into an impeccable ponytail. Her tailored show coat and polished boots spoke of someone who demanded perfection. She pivoted smoothly on her heel to track the rider's progress, reminding me of a hawk watching its prey.

It was a teenage girl on a bay horse who she was staring at so intently. As they approached a single vertical, the girl leaned forward slightly at takeoff, and the horse chipped in, clearing the fence but not smoothly.

"Again!" the woman barked, her tone leaving no room for argument.

Ripley settled beside me, his nose twitching as he surveyed the activity in the ring.

The one yelling has cranky boss energy, he observed.

I bit my cheek to keep from laughing and glanced quickly at Amy, making sure she hadn't noticed me reacting to Ripley's commentary. After decades of keeping my "unusual" ability to myself, hiding my conversations with animals had become second nature.

The rider circled back and approached the jump once

7

more, this time waiting for the jump in a more balanced seat. The horse flowed over the fence with ease.

"Better," the woman called. "Now with more pace and come back to it from the other direction."

"She's intense," I whispered to Amy as we leaned against the rail.

"That's Miranda Caldwell," Amy murmured, folding her arms. "She's an amazing trainer, old school, been around forever, and super demanding. Every single one of her students has perfect position. Look at that lower leg—it's glued in place."

I watched the horse and its rider approach the jump again, their rhythm so smooth it almost looked choreographed.

"It's like watching a masterclass."

"She's trained more champions than anyone else in the state. Many of her students have gone on to ride professionally." Amy's voice dropped slightly. "But she's ruthless about maintaining standards. I heard she dropped three students last month because they weren't serious enough."

The teenager completed another jump, landing with precision before transitioning into a smooth canter.

I watched, mesmerized, as the instructor barked out corrections. Her voice carried across the arena with the sharp precision of someone who'd spent decades molding riders into champions. Even from this distance, I could see how her student responded instantly to her critiques. She reminded me of my high school math teacher—the one who could silence a room with just a raised eyebrow.

I shifted uncomfortably. "Remind me never to ride when she's watching."

"Oh, she watches everyone," Amy said with a grin. "Says

it's her duty to protect the sport's integrity." Her tone carried a mix of respect and wry amusement.

I grimaced, imagining those piercing eyes scrutinizing my far less-than-perfect position. Even from here, I could feel the scrutiny, though she wasn't even looking in my direction. "Protect the sport's integrity" sounded an awful lot like "criticize everyone who isn't perfect."

Amy nudged me as we leaned against the rail. "Come on, let's grab our numbers and then we need to get Belle and Cooper braided."

I followed her reluctantly, glancing over my shoulder at the warm-up ring one last time. Riders seemed to glide through their paces, their horses like dancers who already knew all the steps.

I felt nauseous.

Ripley looked up at me.

If you puke, aim away from me.

~

THE OFFICE BUZZED WITH ACTIVITY. Tall, lanky teenagers lined up at the check-in desk, their mothers fussing over them, adjusting pristine show coats and tucking already perfect hair into their hairnets. Standing behind them, I felt particularly short and particularly wide.

What was I thinking going in a horse show at my age? And what about the very real possibility of falling off? I might end up badly hurt, not to mention making a complete fool of myself in front of everyone—which seemed inevitable at this point.

This was possibly one of my worst decisions ever.

I clutched Ripley's leash tighter, earning a side-eye from

him that clearly said, get it together, human. Amy stood behind me, radiating her usual confidence. If I wasn't friends with her and hadn't seen firsthand how hard she works, I might assume she was one of *them*—the effortlessly perfect riders who glided through the show ring without a trace of doubt.

When it was my turn, I stepped up hesitantly.

"Name?" The woman at the table didn't look up from her stack of numbers.

"Jennifer..." I cleared my throat. "Harlow. Jennifer Harlow."

She glanced up, her efficient movements pausing. Her gaze lingered as she took in my presumably deer-in-the-headlights expression.

"Have fun out there," she said with a quick smile, handing me a number.

"Thanks," I murmured, the kindness catching me off guard, though I cringed at how obvious my fear must be.

I stared down at the bold black 1 3 2 printed on the cardstock. My very first show number. I felt an odd mix of dread and pride.

"I'm so excited you agreed to do this," Amy said with her usual infectious enthusiasm, as she turned to give the woman her name. Her excitement was contagious—even if my nerves weren't on board. Amy had been pushing me to enter a show for months, insisting that Cooper and I were more than ready. "What did you and Liz end up deciding to start you at, cross-rails?"

I shot her a playful glare. "Two-foot, for your information. Some of us are still working our way up to your level of expertise," I teased.

"Experienced hobbyist," Amy countered playfully, draping her arm across my shoulders while we made our way out of the office. "Despite popular opinion, Jen," Amy said as we headed out, "the height of the jumps, like pant sizes, doesn't matter. We're here for fun. And we all had to start somewhere." She squeezed my shoulder. "Now, let's go braid Cooper and Belle before you talk yourself out of this."

The announcer's voice crackled over the loudspeaker, cheerful and slightly too loud. "Good morning, riders! Friendly reminder... it's not about the ribbons—it's about making it through the day with your dignity intact."

I glanced up sharply.

I know, right? Ripley quipped, his ears twitching. *He must know you're here!*

Chapter Two

I stood on a two-step, rug hook tucked in my pocket while I attempted to braid Cooper's mane.

Liz insisted her riders braid their own horses. "If you're going to show, you should know how to do the work yourself," she'd said more than once, her no-nonsense tone leaving no room for argument.

It was admirable, in theory.

In practice, it was just me, Cooper's seemingly endless mane, and a growing sense of frustration.

The gray yarn tangled around my fingers for what must be the tenth time.

"Cross the strands, add the yarn," I muttered, trying to remember the YouTube tutorial I'd watched five times last night. "It's not rocket science."

Cooper turned his head toward me. *You're making this more complicated than necessary.*

Easy for you to say. You just get to stand there looking majestic.

Dignified and tolerant, he corrected, shifting his weight.

Ripley huffed from his spot near the stall door. *Why are you putting string in his hair anyway? Seems unnecessary.*

It's tradition, I told him with a sigh, attempting another braid. The yarn slipped through my fingers again.

"Having fun over there?" Amy's voice drifted over from the next stall.

"Oh yeah, loads. I think I've invented an entirely new style of braid—patent pending."

Cooper flicked an ear back at me. *Stick to the basics, please. I'd like to get back to my hay.*

"You're supposed to be supportive," I muttered under my breath, grabbing another piece of yarn and focusing on the next section of mane.

Cooper flicked an ear.

Amy appeared beside me, her own braiding finished in record time. She grabbed a section of Cooper's mane and a strand of yarn. "Here—try holding the braid tighter near the base as you pull the yarn through. It keeps things from unraveling."

She demonstrated with a few quick motions, creating a perfect braid like it was second nature. "See? Easy once you get the hang of it."

I gave her a weak smile, glancing down at my mangled attempts. "If I get the hang of it, you'll be the first to know."

Listen to the smart lady, Cooper advised. *I'm getting tired of standing here.*

Ripley's head tilted. *At least you're not the only one who looks ridiculous. Amy's horse has purple string in her mane.* He wrinkled his nose. *It does nothing for her coloring.*

I pressed my lips together, resisting the urge to respond. Instead, I busied myself with another braid, determined to make this one look somewhat professional under Amy's watchful eye.

Only thirty more to go, Cooper reminded me helpfully.

I stared at the length of his neck, still mostly unbraided. "Maybe we could start a new trend. The partially braided look. Very avant-garde."

Amy laughed as she leaned against the stall door. "Nice try. Keep going—you'll get faster with practice."

Or slower, Ripley observed, his head resting on his paws. *That last one took seven minutes, and the one before that took six. I counted.*

I bit the inside of my cheek to keep from replying and reached for another section of mane. Hopefully, I'd be finished before my first round of classes started.

❧

FINALLY DONE with Cooper's braids, my fingers aching, I walked beside Amy toward the concession tent, dodging puddles from yesterday's rain. Two teenage girls walked past, leading their perfectly braided horses. I thought back to Cooper's less-than-perfect braids. Yes, I managed to finish them, but I wished Liz had let me pay someone to do them. I felt bad for him. He deserved to be as fancy-looking as these horses were, especially considering he was going to be carting me around for the day.

"Did you see Sarah's round?" one of the perfect girls whispered. "That chip to fence three was awful."

"At least she made it around. Emma totally messed up the combination."

I groaned. "Amy, do you hear them? This is so out of my league. I feel like I've crashed a party I wasn't invited to." My mind flashed to how girls like that would be watching me in the ring later.

14

Mind you, they probably wouldn't even notice me. The joys of getting older.

"Stop that." Amy nudged me with her elbow. "You belong here as much as anyone else. And Cooper's the kind of partner those kids would be lucky to have on their best day. You've got this."

That's true, Ripley agreed, lifting his head. *He'd prefer you, even if you do bounce on his back a lot. You give him lots of treats.*

I glanced down at Ripley and gave him a small smile. *That was almost supportive of you.* He gave a little wink in response.

"And honestly," Amy continued, "so many of the kids these days don't know half of what Liz is teaching you. You're learning everything from the ground up, just like you should be. It might look like it's all about the fancy tack and outfits when you're at a show, but what really matters is how you take care of your horse, and you're already a superstar in that department."

"Awww, Amy, you're going to make me cry, and I don't even have a reason to... yet," I laughed. "What would I do without you?"

"I mean it. I'm proud of you already. It's not easy doing this as an adult."

We joined the coffee line under the white tent, surrounded by the hum of conversation and the occasional whinny from the nearby horses. Liz appeared beside us, a steaming cup already in hand.

"How are the nerves holding up?" she asked, looking me in the eye.

"Oh, you know," I shrugged with a laugh, "just some minor internal panic. Major panic is scheduled for later. But Amy's being a great cheerleader." I shot Amy a grateful smile. "And I did manage to get Cooper braided, at least in theory."

Amy grinned.

"Glad to hear it," Liz nodded. "Just don't forget to breathe in between the panicking. We don't want you passing out before your classes."

I rolled my eyes and laughed.

Coffees in hand, Amy led us to a corner table, and we all sat down. Ripley sniffed under the table for any leftovers. The coffee heated my hands through the paper cup, offering a bit of relief against the cold morning air.

"Oh, there's Tyler Collins," Amy murmured, tilting her head toward a nearby table.

I glanced over. A tall, lean man stood chatting with another trainer, his navy show coat fitting perfectly across his shoulders. Even his hair was perfectly styled. He looked as if he was preparing for a photoshoot instead of a horse show.

"He's got quite the reputation," Amy whispered, leaning in. "His students clean up at every show, even his adult ammies who barely have time to ride. Makes you wonder what his secret is."

Liz took a careful sip of her coffee. "I've heard rumors but..." She shrugged, letting the thought trail off. "It's not my place to speculate about another trainer's methods."

Too shiny, Ripley huffed from under the table. *Like one of those fancy car salesmen. Something's not right there.*

I shifted in my chair, tugging at my sweatpants.

"I wouldn't know either way," I said. "I'm just hoping to stay on and remember my courses today."

You didn't forget my treats, did you? Ripley chimed in, ever so helpfully. *Because that would be the real disaster.*

Before I could respond, the atmosphere in the tent

16

shifted. A woman walked into the tent, exuding an air of authority, coffee thermos in hand. Her gaze fixed on the man Amy had just pointed out, a look of pure distaste twisting her features.

"Shortcuts never last," she said, loud enough for everyone to hear as she went to stand in the concession line. A hush permeated the crowd.

I nearly choked on my coffee. I wasn't used to such blatant hostility. Was this normal for horse shows?

I glanced over at the man. His expression barely changed, but I caught a momentary flicker of tension in his jaw that disappeared in an instant.

Ooh, burn, Ripley snorted. *Someone needs a treat after that takedown.* I stifled a laugh, pressing my lips together to keep from making a sound. Amy and Liz exchanged a wide-eyed look.

"That's Miranda Caldwell," Amy whispered. "Remember her from the warmup area?" I nodded. "Like I told you, she's an amazing trainer but ruthless, and not just with her own students. She'll go after anyone she disagrees with and won't be quiet about it." Amy pretended to shudder. "I'll keep my casual riding status, thanks. Lower stakes, better beverages."

I put my hand over my mouth as I covered my laugh.

"Come on, Amy, you're way better than some casual rider," Liz protested. "Don't sell yourself short."

"Fair enough," Amy conceded with a nod. "Still, I prefer keeping things light and not getting screamed at over mistakes. I'm so grateful you're not that type of instructor, Liz. If you barked orders at me like she does, I'd probably curl up in a ball somewhere and sob. Though I'm curious what she meant by that comment to Tyler," she mused, lifting her brows. "I've heard she's never approved of his methods. Thinks he's all about the ribbons and not the hors-es." Amy shook her head. "Makes you wonder, though."

I took a sip of my coffee. Horse show drama. It was defi-nitely more interesting than I'd expected. The part of me that had devoured horse novels as a kid found it strangely thrilling to witness a real-life rivalry at a horse show unfold.

No sooner had the dust settled from the drama with Tyler and Miranda than my attention was drawn to another table where a well-dressed woman sat talking animatedly. Her clipped voice carried just enough for me to catch snip-pets of the conversation.

"Rachel gets handed those ribbons on a silver platter because of Apollo. That horse does all the work—doesn't mean she's the best rider."

Amy rolled her eyes, clearly having heard the same as me.

"Show moms," she nodded towards the woman. "Always trying to build up their own kids by tearing others down."

"Who is it?" I asked, drawn into the gossip.

"Victoria Grant," Amy said. "She's one of those ambi-tious horse show moms, always pushing for her daughter to win, no matter what."

She smells like hairspray and desperation, Ripley remarked from under the table. I bit back a smile, grateful for his uncanny ability to sum up a person in a single sniff.

Liz chuckled, shaking her head. "Yup, that's one of the reasons why I prefer a more low-key barn. The moms of our girls are competitive, but then there's next-level competitive."

She drained her coffee and stood up. "Speaking of the girls, I've got to get back to them and make sure they're getting tacked up. It's almost time for them to get in the warmup ring." She turned to me and put a hand on my shoulder. "You should probably head over to the hunter ring soon, Jen. Watch a few rounds, get a feel for the course."

A flutter of butterflies erupted in my stomach. The show. Right. I'd almost managed to distract myself enough to forget why I was really here amidst the coffee and glimpses into horse-show politics. Well, not really—but I was good at compartmentalizing when I needed to. It seemed like a useful skill at the moment.

"Good idea," I murmured, pushing back my chair. All this horse show gossip was wonderfully distracting, but I had other things to worry about. First up, learning my first course.

∾

"OKAY, SO FIRST THINGS FIRST," Amy said, steering me toward a large board near the hunter ring entrance. "Course sheets. Essential reading material for the aspiring hunter princess." She pointed to a cluster of papers stapled to the board. "Each class has its own course. See how they're not numbered like in the jumpers?"

"Right, Liz mentioned that," I replied, peering at the diagrams. They looked like a chaotic jumble of lines and shapes to me. My stomach lurched. Remembering courses? On top of everything else? I mean, obviously, I knew I'd have to, but now it was getting real, and my mind was already starting to blank just thinking about it.

"Don't worry, it's not as bad as it looks," Amy reassured me, bless her heart. "Think of it like connecting the dots."

She pointed to the first diagram. "This is your first class. See, they're numbered on here. Your first jump is this diagonal, then around to the judge's line, followed by another diagonal to the outside line, finishing with a single diagonal." She dragged her finger over the route she described on the sheet. "It's only eight jumps, and they all kind of make sense in terms of what's next, like you wouldn't veer off from this one to this one." She made a dramatic gesture, proving her point.

I wasn't so sure it would be so common sense once I was out there.

"And see the little box over there?" she continued, gesturing toward a small, elevated structure on the far side of the ring. "That's where the judge sits, making notes and judging your every move. No pressure."

She can smell your fear from there, Ripley snorted. *Just keep smiling and offer treats. Works every time.*

I couldn't help but give a small smile in his direction.

We moved closer to the ring, where several horses were already soaring over impressively high jumps, at least to me. My palms started to sweat.

"Now, you can't actually walk the course in hunters," Amy explained, "but you can watch the other riders. See how many strides they're putting in between each jump? You'll probably add a stride since your jumps are lower and you won't be going as fast, but it gives you a good idea."

"Add a stride?" I squeaked, my voice barely above a whisper. My brain felt like it was already at maximum capacity. How was I supposed to remember all this *and* ride at the same time? Was my middle-aged brain even up to the task?

Ripley snorted. *Just breathe, Treat Lady. One hoof in front of the other. Or something like that.*

Amy squeezed my arm. "Hey, you've got this. Just focus on one course at a time. Don't try to memorize all of them at once, or you'll get them mixed up."

Memorizing more than one course wasn't even registering with my brain yet, but yes, that was a fact. I had to learn more than one course today. Good grief, what had I gotten myself into?

Amy glanced at her watch. "Yikes, I need to get myself organized. My classes are soon. Let's get this show on the road!" She grinned.

I grimace-smiled in return.

~

BACK AT THE BARN, the familiar scent of hay and horses calmed my nerves a fraction. Amy efficiently tacked up Belle, while I gave Cooper some treats. Nothing wrong with keeping the bribery train going—especially when my nerves needed all the help they could get.

"Don't overthink everything," Amy said, adjusting Belle's saddle. "Just get the general flow. It looks overwhelming, I know. But honestly, if you forget where you're going, Cooper will probably know where to go anyway, he's done this so many times."

"Pretty sure I'm about to humiliate myself," I muttered, my fingers tightening around Ripley's leash. My chest felt too tight, my pulse too fast. My nerves were getting to me. "You've been doing this your whole life. I'm about to make a complete fool of myself in front of everyone." I let out a shaky breath and wiped my palms on my sweats. "Amy, I seriously don't belong here."

Amy's expression softened. "Honey, nobody expects perfection, especially at your first show. Just go out there, have fun, and let Cooper do his thing."

Her reassuring smile should have made me feel better. It almost did.

She's right, you know, Cooper's voice echoed in my

head. *You just need to...well, not fall off. But no big deal if you do, I won't hold it against you.* He nudged my shoulder gently with his nose, his breath warm against my neck. A calming warmth spread through me, steadying my nerves in a way no pep talk ever could.

He really was amazing. How did I get so lucky to have him in my life? I managed to catch his eye, sending him a silent thank you that I hoped he could feel.

What about me, Treat Lady? I'm the one that puts up with you day and night. You just see him a few times a week. Ripley snorted, interrupting the moment.

Right you are, Ripley. I gave him a subtle wink, the tension easing just a bit. *How did I get so lucky to have you too?*

I smiled back at Amy and took a deep breath.

I'd signed up for this. *I wanted this.* I could do this. This was my chance—my crazy, middle-aged dream come true.

And no matter what happened in that ring, I was lucky to be here, surrounded by these amazing creatures, human and otherwise.

The loudspeaker crackled to life, the announcer's voice filled with a mix of encouragement and humor. "Attention, riders! Remember, confidence is key—or at least fake it 'til you make it!"

Amy and I exchanged glances and cracked up. Well, at least the announcer knew their audience.

Chapter Three

"I'll just tidy up Cooper's stall while you're warming up," I told Amy, "then I'll come watch your rounds."

The truth was, I needed something to do—anything to distract myself from the nervous energy buzzing through me. Cleaning stalls was always calming.

After dumping the used shavings into the manure pile, I took the wheelbarrow and headed toward the massive pile of shavings near the back of the stalls. Ripley trotted alongside me, his leash slack, sniffing at the air like he always did.

Then he froze. His ears shot forward, nose twitching. A low growl rumbled from his chest.

I barely had time to react before he lunged, hauling on the leash with unexpected force. I stumbled forward, nearly toppling into the wheelbarrow.

"Ripley, what—?"

He dragged me toward the shavings pile. My pulse kicked up. This wasn't just curiosity—this was something else.

"What is it, Rip?" I asked, my brow furrowing. There was something in his eyes, an intensity that set me on edge.

Something's not right, he huffed. *Over here.*

I swallowed hard and let him pull me forward, my steps hesitant.

Then I saw it.

A shape. Half-buried in the shavings. A person. Face down. Motionless.

My breath hitched, and my hand flew to my mouth. Oh my God.

I inched my way closer. Ripley, no longer pulling on the leash, looked up at me, his big eyes filled with worry.

As I got closer, recognition slammed into me. Miranda Caldwell. The trainer we'd just seen at the concession stand barely an hour ago.

My pulse roared in my ears.

"Ma'am?" I said, my voice wavering, hoping beyond hope she'd just fainted. I leaned down and pressed a hand to her shoulder and gave her a gentle shake. She didn't move, but the moment my skin touched her, a jolt of energy hit me, and a fragmented vision flashed through my mind.

Miranda's face flushed with anger as she argued with someone. Then—just as quickly—it was gone.

For as long as I could remember, the visions had come unbidden. Glimpses of events I couldn't explain, sometimes triggered by touching an object.

I stared down at her, my breath catching in my throat.

"Miranda?" I called her name this time. She still didn't respond.

Reality slammed into me, and before I could stop it, I screamed.

The horses in the stalls nearby startled, lifting their heads, ears swiveling toward the sudden noise. My legs went weak beneath me, and I stumbled back a step.

"Jen? What's wrong?" Liz's voice, sharp with concern,

cut through the fog in my mind. She appeared at my side, her gaze following mine until it landed on Miranda. Her face blanched, her eyes widening.

"Oh my God. Someone call 911!" she shouted while pulling me back, her arm around my shoulders. "Come on, Jen, step back," she said, her voice steady.

People began converging, their faces pale, eyes wide as they took in the scene.

Ripley stood beside me, sniffing the air. He let out a low growl, his eyes sharp.

She smells wrong. Not dead-dead... weird-dead. His voice drifted into my head, his cryptic words sending a shiver down my spine.

Weird-dead? Trust Ripley to find a category for every kind of dead.

I glanced at Liz, her worried gaze meeting mine.

"Jen, are you okay?" she asked gently, her arm still around my shoulders. I shook my head, barely able to form words. Okay? How could I be okay? The super strict trainer —the one Amy had pointed out earlier—was lying dead in a pile of shavings, and Ripley was muttering about "weird-dead". It felt completely surreal, too strange to comprehend.

The vision I'd seen when I touched her flashed through my mind—Miranda's face contorted in anger, arguing with someone.

Who had she been arguing with? And why?

My head spun, everything around me blurring as my mind tried to make sense of it.

"Sit down here," Liz murmured, guiding me to a stack of hay bales. "Just breathe, okay? Stay right here."

I nodded numbly. The hay was scratchy and uncomfortable, but at least it kept me from face-planting onto the barn floor.

I could hear people talking, hushed voices, the occasional gasp. Somewhere, the tinny crackle of the loudspeaker broke through the chaos, announcing something mundane—something about checking in for the next class. It was such an odd contrast to everything happening that I almost laughed.

Ripley nudged my knee, his big eyes full of concern. He was a little sarcastic pocket rocket most of the time, but he also knew when I needed him.

"I'm okay, Rip," I whispered, more to convince myself than him.

"Attention, riders!" The announcer's cheerful voice echoed through the showgrounds, almost jarringly bright, clearly unaware of the unfolding tragedy. "Let's keep those smiles wide—after all, it's just a horse show, not the end of the world!"

I glanced up, a shaky laugh escaping me. The absurdity of it—the cheerful announcement in the midst of everything —was almost too much.

Liz caught my eye, her lips twitching in a faint smile.

"See?" she said softly. "We'll get through this. One step at a time."

I nodded, swallowing hard. She was right, but it felt strange to think about continuing. Would they even hold the show now? Part of me hoped they'd cancel it, give us all time to process what had happened.

But as the announcer's voice crackled overhead again, calling the next class to the ring, I realized that wasn't going to happen.

Somehow, despite everything, the world—especially the horse show world—just kept turning.

THE WAIL of sirens had long since faded, but the ambulance still idled nearby, its back doors hanging open. A paramedic crouched beside Miranda's still form, speaking in low tones to the uniformed officer standing nearby. The other was on the radio, presumably confirming what little they knew.

I sat stiffly on the hay bale Liz had pulled me onto, Ripley pressed against my leg. The voices around me felt distant, as though I was listening through water.

A firm voice cut through the fog.

"Detective Hayes."

I blinked up at a tall man approaching. His salt-and-pepper hair and sharp blue eyes gave him the air of someone who had seen it all. He moved with purpose, flipping open a notepad as he stopped in front of us.

His gaze flicked between me and Liz. "I was told one of you found her?"

Liz squeezed my shoulder gently and nodded. "Yes, Jen did."

His attention landed fully on me. "Ms...?"

"Harlow," I managed, my throat dry. "Jennifer Harlow."

He made a note. "Tell me exactly what happened."

I swallowed hard. "I... I was getting shavings for my horse. My dog—" I glanced down at Ripley, who was staring intently at the detective. "—he pulled me to the shavings pile. I couldn't tell it was a person at first, but then... I saw her."

Hayes gave a small nod, his expression unreadable. "Did you touch her?"

"I shook her shoulder a little," I admitted. "She didn't respond." I grimaced at the memory.

The paramedic glanced up from where she knelt beside Miranda. "No obvious signs of trauma."

Hayes hummed, jotting something down. Then he crouched near Miranda, his gaze scanning her still form. The moment stretched. Then he exhaled and stood, tucking his notepad away.

"No obvious signs of foul play," he said. "Could have been a heart attack. Maybe a stroke."

My stomach twisted.

It wasn't impossible. People got worked up, their blood pressure spiked—it happened. And Miranda had been furious. I could still see her face flushed with anger. Maybe it had been enough to push her over the edge.

But then Ripley's voice echoed in my head.

Weird-dead.

A chill prickled up my spine. Not just dead. Weird-dead.

"Are you sure?"

I didn't mean to speak but the words were out before I could stop them.

Hayes's gaze snapped to me, his blue eyes sharpening slightly.

"Ma'am?" His tone shifted, more curious now. "What makes you think otherwise?"

I bit my lip.

How could I tell him about the vision? That I had *seen* her arguing before she died? That my *dog* had somehow sensed something off?

He'd think I was crazy. Or worse—just a middle-aged woman with an overactive imagination.

I glanced down at Ripley, who sat beside me, staring intently at the detective. He let out a short huff, his nose twitching.

Hayes noticed me looking at Ripley. Something in his expression shifted as he watched me exchange glances with my dog, like he was recategorizing me from 'potential witness' to 'eccentric pet owner.'

I hesitated. "He's... very intuitive."

Hayes studied me for a beat longer before tucking his notepad into his pocket.

"The coroner will confirm the cause of death," he said. "But in cases like this, it's usually medical. Things can happen when you least expect it. Even to people who seem healthy."

I glanced at Ripley, who sat beside me, his head cocked, staring intently at Detective Hayes. He let out a soft snort, then looked back at me, his big brown eyes filled with knowing.

Ripley's eyes met mine. *He doesn't see it. But she's weird-dead.*

~

BACK AT COOPER'S STALL, the world seemed to tilt slightly around me. My hands trembled as I fumbled to push the stall door open. Once inside, Cooper nudged my shoulder, his warm breath a comforting anchor. Ripley trotted in behind me, settling near my feet with a concerned whine.

Easy, Jen, Cooper murmured, his voice a low rumble in my mind. *Just breathe.*

I leaned my forehead against his neck and closed my eyes. Breathe in, breathe out. Breathe in, breathe out.

Detective Hayes's words echoed in my head. Natural causes. Just a heart attack. Part of me wanted desperately to believe that. He was the professional, after all. What did I know? But the vision I'd had gnawed at me. And then there was what Ripley said. How could I just forget about those things and go on with my day?

A sharp voice cut through the quiet. *Are you always this quick to ignore your instincts, or is it just when a man in authority tells you to?*

My eyes snapped open.

Cooper's head shot up, ears pricked forward.

Standing before me was Miranda Caldwell—translucent, shimmering, and looking thoroughly annoyed. She glanced around the stall, a flicker of uncertainty crossing her face before she masked it with her usual stern expression.

Wonderful, she said, *of all the people who could see me, it had to be the middle-aged amateur wearing sweatpants.*

Well, this is... unexpected, Cooper said. *As if we didn't have enough to deal with today.*

Miranda's form flickered. *I'm sorry, is my death inconveniencing your show schedule?* Her voice wavered slightly on the word "death". *I've been trying to get someone's attention for the past hour, and apparently you,* she looked me up and down, *are the only one who can see me.*

I pressed back harder against Cooper. The ghost of a hyper-critical trainer coming to haunt me at my first horse show? Yeah, sure. Why not? That was the kind of day I was having.

Oh for heaven's sake, she snapped, arms crossed, *someone murdered me, and while you're standing there gawking, my killer is probably packing up their trailer.*

Cooper snorted, tossing his head. *Who does she think she is?* he said, his voice clear in my mind. *You shouldn't have to deal with this, Jen. I know who she is. I've seen her make many of her students cry over the years. I do not want her doing that to you. And we've got a show to worry about.*

Ripley shifted uneasily at my feet. *But Cooper, the cranky boss lady is right,* he said, his tone unusually earnest. *She's weird-dead, not dead-dead. Someone killed her.*

Cooper shifted slightly to look back at me and then to Ripley. *But she's mean to people, Ripley. Jen doesn't deserve that, and she's got enough to worry about today. I'd really like her to not fall off.* He glanced over at me, concern evident in his kind eyes.

Well, that was kind of him, though I was a bit annoyed with how little faith he had in me.

Enough pandering, Miranda screeched. *You think this is up for debate? She is the only one who can see me, which means she's the only one who can do something. So suck it up, Jennifer. You've got the intuition and apparently a pint-sized partner-in-crime. And I'm sure your horse can cart you around your little hunter courses.*

Cooper sighed. *Well, she's not wrong. I'll leave it to you, Jen.*

Ripley, who had been watching Miranda with wary eyes, glanced at me, then back at her. *I told you. We have to find out what really happened.*

I reached down to scratch behind his ears.

"Of course, this would happen today," I muttered. "My first horse show, and instead of worrying about remembering my courses and staying on Cooper, I'm getting bossed around by a ghost."

And now I was supposed to solve said ghost's murder?

Miranda gave an exasperated huff. *The longer you wait,* she said, *the colder the trail gets. Everyone's going to assume I had a stroke or heart attack just because I wasn't all butterflies and rainbows. You're the only one who knows the truth. Are you going to help me or not?*

I swallowed hard, feeling the pressure of Miranda's expectant gaze.

"But I'm not a detective," I answered, shaking my head. "How can I possibly figure out what happened to you? All

I've got is a vision of you arguing with someone and now this." I gestured to her standing in front of me.

I'll help, Jen. Ripley said, his little face a picture of determination. *I can sniff things out, and maybe trip people to get them to talk. They won't see me coming.*

I laughed. "I'm not sure that's quite what will do it, but I appreciate the sentiment, Rip." I leaned down and gave him a rub on the head.

Cooper let out a big sigh. *You know I'll support you either way, Jen, but if you do it, make sure you don't let her push you around. We've worked hard for this, and you deserve to enjoy your first show. Well, as best you can while wanting to throw up, that is.* He gave me a playful nudge with his nose.

Miranda scowled at Cooper. *Are you done babysitting her yet?*

Cooper flattened his ears and tossed his head at her. Miranda stood her ground, unfazed.

"I don't know if I can do this," I said, my voice barely above a whisper, "but I suppose I have to try. If I don't and there's a killer out there, they might get away with it, and they might even kill someone else."

That's right, Jen, Ripley chimed in. *It's up to us.*

Who knew his secret goal in life was to be a detective?!

Cooper snorted softly, his support evident even though I knew he was worried about me.

"All right," I finally said, my voice firmer now as I squared my shoulders. "I'll do it."

Miranda gave a curt nod, the barest hint of a smile tugging at her lips before she began to fade. *Don't waste time, Jennifer. They'll be gone by the end of the show, if not before. You need to find out who did this to me before they leave.*

And then she was gone.

Cooper nudged my shoulder again, and I smiled faintly, reaching up to scratch his neck. "Looks like we're in it now, huh, boy?" He snorted.

Ripley huffed in agreement.

I took a deep breath. Apparently, this was happening. Because clearly just not falling off today wasn't going to be challenging enough.

"Well, kids," I said, as bravely as I could manage, "we've got a murder to solve—and a horse show to ride in!"

Ripley gave me a classic Boston Terrier grin, and Cooper sagely nodded his head. They were in.

Chapter Four

So... *what now?* I asked my new detective team, glancing between the two of them.

Cooper flicked an ear toward me. *Just start with anything suspicious. The truth will follow. It's not as complicated as you're making it.*

His reaction was so typical of his steady personality—exactly why he was such a pro in the hunter ring, especially for Nervous Nellies like me.

Ripley lifted his head, tilting it sharply in that way he did when he was considering something. *Truth, justice, and snacks for all. Let's get moving, Treat Lady. Weird-Dead Lady is counting on you.*

And there was the go-getter Ripley, always ready for an adventure.

Between the two of them, I just might have a chance of staying sane—and finding Miranda's killer.

I gave them both a look. *I appreciate the encouragement, really, but people don't just walk around spilling clues like breadcrumbs.*

Shows what you know, Ripley sniffed. *People talk all the time. You just don't listen properly.*

I rolled my eyes. *Okay, so how do you propose I listen properly?*

Ripley did his own version of an eye roll right back at me. I didn't even know that was possible. *Weird-Dead Lady had enemies,* he said, like he was stating the obvious. *Find out who they are and then go listen to what they're saying.*

Cooper swished his tail lazily. *He's right. You'll hear who had motive if you pay attention.*

You two should open a detective agency. You seem to have it all figured out.

I swear they both shrugged in agreement.

So you're saying I'm just supposed to eavesdrop?

Not just eavesdrop—snoop, sniff, and sleuth, Ripley declared, tilting his head sharply to emphasize each word like a professor giving a lecture.

Cooper's warm breath brushed my shoulder as he nudged me gently. *You already know how to do this. Just listen.*

How is it that animals are so wise, I wondered, while humans are so... not?

I took a breath. *Okay, I get it. Let's start at the beginning. What do we know so far?*

Ripley sat back on his haunches, his head tilting thoughtfully. *We know Miranda is weird-dead, not normal-dead. We know she's bossy even in the afterlife. And we know you're already in the middle of this, so no backing out.*

Great. That tells me absolutely nothing. I paused, considering his earlier suggestions about listening for clues. *Though I have to admit, your idea about finding her enemies isn't bad.*

Of course, it isn't, Ripley sniffed. *Now can we go snoop or what?*

The barn's PA system crackled to life, the announcer's voice breaking through the quiet. "Attention, riders! Hunter warm-ups are in progress. And for those keeping score at home, we're currently running fifteen minutes behind schedule and about three emotional breakdowns ahead. Just another day in paradise, folks."

∾

WHAT A WORLD, Miranda's voice drawled behind me as I walked, sending a shiver down my spine.

I turned to find her standing just behind me, a scowl on her face.

You'd think someone would at least pretend to care, she continued, her translucent form shimmering faintly. *But no, it's all business as usual. Shows where their priorities lie, doesn't it?*

I hesitated, unsure how to respond.

People probably just don't know how to process it, I said finally.

Miranda raised an eyebrow. *Don't make excuses for them, Jennifer. People are who they are. It's why I always preferred horses over people.*

Ripley sniffed the air. *I think Weird-Dead Lady is right. She may have been rude, but they could at least pretend to care.*

You all have a point, Cooper's voice chimed in. *But people often don't know what to do when someone dies. And horse shows can bring out the worst in some people. Or the best. All depends on the person.*

Their voices swirled in my mind, an odd comfort amid

the chaos, which I appreciated. Still, it was time to get to work.

Alright, everyone, I announced, straightening my posture and taking a deep breath. *I appreciate what you're all saying, but let's stop dwelling on people's lack of empathy. I need all of you to pitch in if we're going to solve this before the day is over. If we don't, Miranda's killer will get away with it.*

With Ripley's leash in hand, I strode down the aisle with determination. Amy's rounds were starting soon, and I didn't want to miss them. At the same time, I'd keep my ears open. If there was anything to pick up about who had it out for Miranda, I wasn't about to miss that either.

As I passed the last stall and rounded the corner, I caught sight of a well-dressed woman gesturing animatedly to another woman as they stood in front of a show barn's lounge tent. Something about her seemed familiar.

"...completely unfair. The judges always favor riders like her. It's ridiculous."

The memory clicked into place. Amy had pointed her out earlier—Victoria Grant, the show mom who'd been complaining at the concession stand about another rider always winning.

The other woman murmured something I couldn't make out, but Victoria's response was loud and clear. "Of course they do! You think it's her talent? Please. It's that horse. That's the only reason she wins."

I stepped closer, trying to look like I was simply passing by, but Victoria's sharp gaze snapped to me. Her lips thinned, her expression icy.

"Can I help you?" Her voice dripped artificial sweetness. "Or are you just here to stick your nose where it doesn't belong?"

Caught off guard, I stammered, "Oh, no. I was just—"

"Eavesdropping?" Victoria cut in, her tone accusatory. Her sharp gaze flicked over me with open disdain.

The accusation hit me like a slap. "I... I wasn't eavesdropping," I stammered, the words tumbling out awkwardly.

Victoria raised an eyebrow, her mouth tightening as she looked me over like I was something she'd scraped off her boot. "Maybe you should mind your own business."

Her words lingered as she brushed past me, motioning to the woman she was with to follow her. My cheeks burned, a mix of anger and humiliation bubbling beneath the surface. The way she dismissed me so easily struck a nerve, making me painfully aware of how out of place I already felt at the show.

Well, isn't she charming, Ripley muttered, his nose twitching as he watched her go. *Hiding something or just nasty? Toss-up, really.*

She's got a reputation, Miranda said, appearing suddenly at my side. *Always has. Ambition oozes out of her like cheap perfume. Her poor kid is a decent rider but with a mother like that? I wouldn't train her no matter how much her mother paid me.*

I hesitated, glancing back toward the path Victoria had taken. She'd been overly defensive and rude, but that could just be the kind of person she was. Then again, Ripley and Miranda might be right—maybe there was something more to it.

Do you think she knows something? I asked.

Miranda tilted her head, her expression unreadable. *If she does, good luck getting it out of her. Victoria only cares about one thing—winning. And she doesn't care who she steps on to get there.*

Ripley snorted. *She's hiding something. Bet my kibble on it.*

I sighed. Was she? Victoria's defensiveness was odd, but did it really have anything to do with Miranda?

"Come on," I whispered. "Let's go watch Amy's rounds before we draw any more attention to ourselves."

Ripley trotted ahead, his little legs moving with purpose. Miranda lingered for a moment, her gaze following Victoria before she vanished with a faint shimmer.

❧

THE HUNTER RING hummed with quiet energy, the rhythm of hooves on packed sand blending with the low murmur of trainers coaching. Along the rail, riders in polished boots and pristine show coats watched intently.

Ripley trotted beside me, his head swiveling to take in the activity. *This place is fascinating. So many people pretending to be calm while their insides are a mess.*

Amy spotted me from the in-gate and waved. She sat tall on Belle, her bay mare, who flicked her ears toward the ring as if eager to get started. Liz stood nearby, her sharp eyes focused on the rider in the ring.

"She's ready," Liz said as I joined her. "Belle is looking solid today."

"She looks calm," I said, watching Amy gather her reins.

Liz smiled. "She's good under pressure. Not that she doesn't get nervous, but she channels it well."

"Wish I could do that," I admitted, though between a murder, a ghost, and, you know, being in my first horse show, it felt nearly impossible.

Amy glanced back at us with a quick grin before urging

Belle into the ring. Liz leaned forward slightly, her focus intense.

Belle moved into a smooth canter, her stride even and steady. Amy guided her toward the first fence, her hands quiet and her posture relaxed. They flowed over the jump with ease, staying in perfect rhythm.

Not bad, Miranda appeared next to me, arms crossed as she observed, *but her hands are stiff, and the horse is a touch lazy with her front legs over the jumps.*

I froze. She glanced at me, raising an eyebrow. *Don't look so shocked. I may be dead, but I still know what I'm talking about.*

I quickly averted my gaze, focusing back on Amy. I wasn't surprised by Miranda showing up or her critique—I mean, it's Miranda—but I was hoping Liz hadn't noticed my expression. Miranda's sudden appearances were unnerving, and her blunt commentary about Amy wasn't helping.

And I thought Amy was doing amazing, but what did I know?

I didn't need to worry. Liz didn't take her eyes off Amy, completely absorbed in her round. "See how she's keeping a steady rhythm and then going right to the rail after her jumps, not cutting any corners? That's what the judges love in the hunters. You want to make it look easy."

Easy for her to say.

Your coach is right. That's one of the many goals in hunters, but it takes countless other details as well to get it all right, Miranda said, watching Amy as intently as Liz.

Blah, blah, blah. I told you she's a bossy one, Ripley humphed at my feet.

And remember who you're riding, Cooper chimed in. *I've got it covered. Been there, done that.*

Ripley sniffed the air and glanced at me. *He's not wrong, but jeez, arrogant much?*

A soft chuckle echoed in my head.

I bit my lip, a laugh threatening to escape—likely the first sign of delirium. What on earth was my life turning into today? Cooper and Ripley nattering away, and now a ghost with running commentary about my friend's hunter round. At least they were helping keep my nerves at bay.

Amy completed her round with a smooth final fence, bringing Belle back to a quiet trot before leaving the ring, a big smile on her face as she approached the in-gate.

"Well done!" Liz called, clapping softly. "That was beautiful."

"Yes, that was amazing, Amy!" I called.

Amy led Belle toward us. "She was fantastic out there," she said, her cheeks flushed with excitement.

Liz nodded. "You were both fantastic. You can get off for a bit now since your next class won't be for a while."

Ripley tilted his head, his nose twitching. *Wow, such skill. Truly a marvel. Now, if only they could do it while holding a tennis ball in their mouths—but okay, good job, Belle and Amy.*

Belle snorted, flicking an ear in Ripley's direction.

I stifled a laugh, shaking my head. *You're impossible.*

At least your friend earned her compliments, Miranda smirked. *Some of the riders here are just passengers with expensive horses and trainers who take shortcuts.*

I frowned, unsure what she meant, but before I could ask, Liz checked her watch and gestured toward the warm-up ring. "Your classes will be in a few hours, Jen. Plan to start tacking up about an hour before. That'll give us time to give you a good warm-up."

I felt my stomach tighten at the reminder of my looming horse show debut. "Got it," I said, trying to sound calm.

"I'd better head back to the kids. You okay for a bit?"

"Yeah, I'm fine," I said, keeping my tone light. "I think I'll wander over to the concession stand. Maybe grab some coffee and then check on Cooper."

Liz nodded, already focused on her next task. I watched her walk away, then turned my attention toward the bustling concession area.

Ripley gave me a knowing look, his ears twitching. *Coffee. Right. Definitely not snooping.*

Chapter Five

*W*e're *blending in perfectly. Totally inconspicuous,*
Ripley quipped as we approached the concession.

"Uh-huh," I murmured, pretending to study the menu
while keeping tuned to the conversations swirling around
me. If anything useful was being said, I didn't want to
miss it.

"She always had a holier-than-thou attitude," a voice cut
through the din, grabbing my attention.

Another voice chimed in, softer but no less cutting. "She
wasn't wrong, though. Everyone knows Tyler takes shortcuts. There's no way his students could win as much as they
do otherwise. Miranda just had the nerve to call him out
on it."

I paused. Tyler? Shortcuts? Amy had mentioned him
earlier, something about wondering what his winning secret
was. And Miranda had made some snarky remark at the
concession earlier. Now his name was cropping up again
along with Miranda's?

Were they implying he might have done something
to her?

Miranda appeared beside me, her translucent form pacing in a restless loop. I must be getting used to her sudden appearances. I didn't even jump this time.

He's always been slippery, she muttered. *Cutting corners, bending rules. It's no secret I called him out more than once. But today specifically?* She stopped abruptly, shaking her head. *I can't remember. It's like a fog whenever I try to think about what happened. Maybe I hit my head. Or maybe it's just because I'm dead.*

She let out a frustrated sigh and shimmered faintly. *People like Tyler with all their dirty secrets don't like to be challenged though.*

I gave her a quick glance. *So, do you think he's the one who killed you?*

She pursed her lips. *Let's just say I wouldn't be surprised if he wanted me gone.*

My mind churned, processing what I'd heard so far. If Miranda had called Tyler out for shady training practices, it sounded like he might have a motive... Maybe he was the killer. Could solving her murder be that easy?

Sounds like the gossipy ladies wouldn't be surprised if he did it. Ripley's nose twitched as he glanced toward the women at the picnic table. *Why not just ask what they know?*

Not exactly how this works, buddy, I replied.

The women's conversation shifted, moving on to schedules and classes, as if they hadn't just implied Tyler might have killed Miranda.

Miranda huffed beside me. *Typical,* she muttered. *Whispering behind backs, hinting at secrets, but never saying it outright. Cowards. They'd rather gossip than actually do anything, even when they know it's wrong.*

Ripley snorted. *Humans are weird. And self-absorbed.*

It seems you're not wrong. I sighed. *I think that's all we're going to get from here.*

Ahead, Detective Hayes caught my attention. He was standing near the show office, scanning the area as he spoke with a uniformed officer. His posture was relaxed, but his focus looked razor-sharp.

Miranda paused, her expression shifting from frustration to a faint smirk. *Looks like your detective isn't completely sold on the 'natural causes' theory.*

Ripley tilted his head, his ears twitching. *Or maybe he's just hanging around because he likes the food truck.*

Miranda snorted. *Whatever his reasons, don't count on him to figure this out before the murderer's long gone. Let's be real—if anyone's solving this, it's you.*

I let out a dry chuckle, immediately bringing up my hand to hide it. *Well, I'll need more evidence than a ghost, some visions, and gossip at the concession.*

Don't forget about your trusty companion and steady steed, Ripley quipped. *You'd be nothing without us.*

A vision of a bucketful of carrots popped into my mind. Cooper. Of course.

I bit back a laugh, grateful for the brief levity. *You're right. Full credit to the team. And yes, Ripley, you'll get your treats. Cooper, you'll get all the carrots too.*

Cooper's warm chuckle filled my mind. *Good answer.*

Ripley huffed, his tone mock-indignant. *And they say humans don't understand us.*

Ripley's nose twitched suddenly, and his head snapped toward the stalls. *Something interesting over there,* he said, tugging insistently at his leash. *I can feel it.*

I hesitated, glancing between him and Miranda. His gaze was sharp, his little body vibrating with purpose.

Miranda raised an eyebrow. *I'd listen to him if I were you. He's got better instincts than most people.*

All right, lead the way, Rip.

~

RIPLEY'S EARS FLICKED FORWARD, his nose working overtime as he wove through the crowded aisle. The chaos of riders and horses didn't faze him—he was on a mission.

"What are you onto now, Rip?" I whispered, glancing around to make sure no one was paying us too much attention. This was giving a horrible sense of déjà vu. I really hoped I wasn't about to stumble onto another dead body.

Ripley stopped suddenly, his eyes glued to an open stall near the end of the aisle. He then ran forward, making me stumble as he hauled me forward.

Scrambling to my feet, we made our way into the stall. Everything looked ordinary at first glance. A neat pile of hay sat in the corner. A deep bed of fresh shavings was spread evenly across the floor.

Ripley sniffed intently along the base of the stall wall, his nose brushing the wood as he tracked a scent upward. I followed his gaze and spotted it. A metal thermos rested on the ledge. It was dulled by scratches, but I could make out a faint engraving of "M.C." on the side. My stomach flipped.

M.C.—Miranda Caldwell. It had to be hers!

Yes, that's mine, Miranda said, her voice tight as she appeared beside me. *I set it there while I was doing the stall. I remember putting it down, but everything after that is a blur.*

Ripley huffed softly, his head tilting as he glanced between me and the thermos. Slowly, I reached out. The cool metal thermos felt light in my hand, then everything around me seemed to dissolve into an eerie silence.

A vision formed.

A hand unscrewed the thermos lid, and a small vial tipped, liquid spilling in with a faint splash. Just as quickly as it came, the vision vanished, and the stall came back into focus.

I squeezed my eyes shut, trying to will the vision to come back, to see more.

You saw something, didn't you? Miranda asked.

I nodded, swallowing hard. *Yes, someone tampered with your coffee. I couldn't see who, but someone definitely put something in your thermos.* I shook my head and sighed. *But that's all I saw. I don't know why everything has to be so cryptic!*

Her lips pressed into a thin line. *I knew it*, she said, her voice tight. *I felt off while I was doing the stall...*

I looked down at the thermos in my hands, suddenly hyperaware of my fingerprints on the metal. *They'll think I did it!* My throat tightened, panic bubbling in my chest.

I glanced around, half expecting someone to appear and accuse me on the spot.

Miranda sighed, folding her translucent arms. *Relax, Jennifer. Nobody's slapping cuffs on you just because you found my coffee thermos, even if someone did poison me.*

I glared at her, my chest tightening further. *But I found it, and now my fingerprints are all over it. Isn't that what happens in every crime show ever?*

She floated closer, her expression softening slightly. *This isn't TV, Jen. No one's arresting you for finding a thermos. The important thing is getting it to someone who will actually do something about it.*

I swallowed hard, her words barely registering through the pounding of my heart. *Okay, fine,* I nodded, clutching the thermos tighter. My legs felt like jelly as I turned toward the aisle. *Let's hope you're right though, and my first horse show doesn't end with me in handcuffs instead of riding Cooper.*

Miranda rolled her eyes and looked at Ripley. *Oh, please. Is she always this dramatic?*

It really is amazing what we put up with, Ripley agreed sagely.

Yes, we do what we must to keep her in check, Cooper's voice chimed in.

The PA system crackled, the announcer's upbeat voice echoing down the aisle. "Attention, riders! Classes for the 3' in the hunter ring are starting soon. And remember, folks—the trick to looking graceful is pretending you've got it all under control... even when you don't!"

Ripley glanced back at me with his usual Boston grin. *He's so spot on every time.*

~

DETECTIVE HAYES WAS STILL near the show office when I spotted him talking with the same uniformed officer.

Honestly, I was surprised he was still here. Miranda's body had already been taken away.

Maybe there was a chance he was looking more into things.

But then I remembered his dismissal of my concerns that she didn't die of natural causes. My heart pounded in my chest, and I clutched the thermos tighter.

All I had to do was give him the thermos, he could get it tested, find out Miranda had been poisoned, and then do whatever investigating beyond that himself. Then I could get back to just stressing about showing and be done with all this "investigating", or whatever you called what I was doing.

How I was going to convince him he needed to test the thermos was something I was choosing not to think about.

Ripley trotted beside me, his head high and his steps purposeful. He tilted his head up at me, his expression amused. *You look like you're trying to talk yourself out of this. Too late for that, Treat Lady.*

"I'm not talking myself out of it," I muttered under my breath. "Just trying to figure out what to say without sounding crazy."

Newsflash—You're going to sound crazy no matter what. Might as well own it.

Detective Hayes's gaze shifted in my direction, and I froze mid-step. His sharp blue eyes met mine, a flicker of recognition crossing his face. He said something to the officer, who nodded and stepped away before turning his full attention toward me.

"Ms. Harlow," he said, his tone polite but curious. "What can I do for you?"

I hesitated, holding up the thermos. "I... I found this. It's Miranda Caldwell's, and I thought... well, I thought you might want it."

His brows furrowed. "A coffee thermos?"

"Yes," I said, my voice steadier now. "It was sitting on the divider in one of her horse's stalls."

"You think this is connected to her death?"

I nodded. "Yes, I do." I couldn't tell him why, but maybe if I acted sure, he'd just go with it. "I really don't think she died of natural causes. I just... have a feeling something's not right."

There, I said it. A little wishy-washy, but I said it.

He studied me, his expression thoughtful. "As I mentioned earlier, sudden deaths don't always make sense at first, but they're usually something medical, an undiagnosed condition or cardiac event."

"I know," I said quickly. "But it just feels off. Like there's more to it."

His lips twitched faintly, almost a smile. "Feels off, huh? Not exactly hard evidence."

Ripley tilted his head, studying Hayes with those big, knowing eyes. *He's skeptical, but hey, at least he doesn't think you're completely nuts. Small victories.*

I ignored Ripley, forcing myself to meet Hayes's steady gaze. "I just thought you'd want to have it. In case."

He nodded and took the thermos, his movements deliberate but casual. My stomach clenched as I watched him handle it barehanded, no gloves or evidence bag in sight.

Ripley humphed. *No gloves? Yeah, looks like he's taking this real seriously.*

Hayes unscrewed the lid and took a careful sniff. His expression remained neutral as he replaced the lid. "Okay, thanks. But unless something obvious comes up, there's not much more I can do."

I nodded, trying not to let the disappointment show, though I wasn't sure what more I expected. "I understand. I just didn't want to let it go."

He handed me a card, his fingers brushing mine briefly in the exchange. "If you notice anything else—anything concrete—call me."

Or maybe he was taking me seriously, at least a little bit.

"Thank you," I said, my voice steadier now.

Hayes hesitated for a moment, his gaze lingering on me before he gave a small nod and turned back toward the show office. His professionalism was unwavering, but there was a subtle warmth in his tone that left me feeling less like an overreacting bystander and more like someone he was willing to listen to—at least a little bit.

Ripley grinned up at me, his eyes gleaming with mischief. *Not bad, Treat Lady. He didn't laugh in your face. Progress.*

Chapter Six

My shoulders felt lighter as I headed back to the hunter ring. I'd done my part. It was in Hayes's hands now.

Cooper's steady voice nudged into my thoughts. *You seem more relaxed. Feeling good about it?*

I smiled as I walked. *Yeah, at least someone's looking into it.*

Someone, sure, Miranda's sharp tone cut in as she shimmered into view beside me. Her arms crossed as she shot me a look. *But don't kid yourself, Jennifer. Just because you handed over the thermos doesn't mean Hayes is going to solve this before the murderer is long gone. That coffee might not get tested for days—if it even gets tested at all.*

The weight settled back onto my shoulders like a lead blanket. *Thanks for that, Miranda. Really helpful.* I let out a frustrated sigh. *Just when I was starting to relax a bit. You know, it'd be nice if I could just focus on attempting to not make a fool of myself at my first horse show.*

Miranda raised an eyebrow, unimpressed. *Quit your complaining, Jennifer. You think I wanted this to happen? I was murdered earlier today, in case you've forgotten, and now I'm haunting an amateur rider who is my only hope for justice.*

Ripley let out a low huff. *She's not wrong, Treat Lady. All you have to do is sit on Cooper and let him do all the work. She's a walking zombie now.*

Miranda's mouth gaped open. *How rude.*

And you saw the detective, Ripley continued, ignoring Miranda. *No gloves, no urgency. I wouldn't exactly call that inspired detective work.*

Thanks, Ripley, I said. *I could use a little more support. Ever heard of "don't bite the hand that feeds you?"*

I swear his big eyes rolled back in his head.

I pursed my lips and shook my head as I walked, veering over to the warm-up ring. I didn't want to be in the midst of this "conversation" once I got to Amy and Liz. *So what are you both saying? That I need to keep investigating?*

Miranda raised an eyebrow. *What I'm saying is, if you don't keep digging, no one will. Hayes is probably filing this under natural causes and moving on.*

Cooper's voice came through, steady and calm. *Unfortunately, she's probably right, Jen. He was polite about it and took the thermos, but he doesn't really have a reason to test it. Feelings don't count for much in the human world.*

Arggh. Okay, fine. I exhaled, shaking off the frustration bubbling under my skin. I leaned on the warm-up ring rail, attempting to look like I was watching the riders.

Humor me for a second then while I break it down. Here's what we know. Miranda, you collapsed in the shavings pile. You had a heated argument with someone. Ripley led me to your thermos, and I saw a vision of someone spiking your coffee. So far, everything points to foul play. Tyler seems like a solid suspect, but is there anyone else you can think of who might have had a grudge against you?

Miranda sighed, crossing her arms again. *I can't recall anything specific. I know I could be... outspoken, let's say, when it came to protecting the horses. Maybe I should've been more diplomatic, but that's never been my style.* She paused, then added with a sniff, *Worked for me—until it didn't.*

Ripley tilted his head, his brown eyes sharp with curiosity. *So, what's the next move?*

I couldn't help but chuckle. As if I knew, but if I didn't laugh, I'd cry.

All right, team. Here's what we're going to do. Ripley, keep doing what you do best—sniffing out trouble and dragging me toward it. Miranda, you keep hovering and judging —maybe you'll notice something the rest of us miss. And Cooper, if your equine network picks up on anything, let me know.

A wry grin spread across Miranda's face. *My, my, look who's stepping up to take charge. Nice to see you dropping the timid, anxious act.*

Ripley let out a mock huff of indignation. *Took you long enough, Treat Lady. I've been carrying this investigation on my back.*

Cooper chuckled in my mind, the sound steady and comforting. *Just remember who's in charge when we hit the ring later. No letting this mystery distract you from your job as my pilot.*

The PA system crackled to life, drawing my attention. The announcer's cheerful voice filled the air. "Attention, riders! Remember—warm-up rings are for everyone, so share the space! And a special shoutout to the rider in the unicorn socks. Bold choice in a place where everyone's trying to look the same!"

Ripley let out a soft snort. *He certainly has a knack for dropping little human truth bombs wrapped in humor.*

∾

WORRIED I'D MISS the rest of Amy's rounds, I hurried back to the hunter ring, Ripley running alongside me. This whole investigating thing wasn't making me a very supportive friend.

As I approached, I could see Amy on Belle by the in-gate, waiting for her turn. She spotted me and waved, her smile bright and confident.

"Glad you made it!" Amy called out. "Just in time!"

I waved back, trying to catch my breath. "I'm so sorry I didn't make it back sooner!" I gestured toward my stomach. "Nerves!" I didn't want to lie but didn't know what else to say. Amy was such a good friend, and I'd barely seen her today. I felt awful.

"No worries. I totally get it," Amy said, her usual sweet and understanding self. She turned her attention back to Belle and gave her a reassuring pat on the neck. Liz stood nearby.

"Remember, stay relaxed and keep your rhythm steady," Liz said, her voice calm but firm.

Amy nodded, taking a deep breath as she prepared to enter the ring. I watched her with admiration, wishing I could borrow some of her confidence for my own upcoming classes.

"Glad you made it back in time for her last round," Liz said. She gestured toward Amy. "She's been doing great today—super consistent rounds. She even won her first class."

I was glad Liz didn't question me about where I was. I didn't want to lie, but what would I say? Miranda didn't die of natural causes, Ripley sniffed out the murder weapon, and now Miranda was haunting me until I found the killer. Maybe eventually I'd tell Liz and Amy about my "gifts," but today wasn't the day.

"I'm so sorry I missed it," I said instead, keeping my eyes on Amy. "But I'm glad I made it for this one."

Belle picked up a smooth canter. Her stride was so rhythmic it looked effortless.

"Belle's got such a nice rhythm," Liz said, echoing my thoughts. "Amy's worked hard for that. And Belle is worth her weight in gold, but Amy's really brought her along beautifully."

I leaned my elbows on the rail and tried to soak in the calm confidence radiating from Amy. "She makes it look so easy."

Liz nodded. "That's what makes a great hunter round— making it look effortless. But there's a lot going on behind the scenes to get there. Don't worry, though—you'll get the hang of it. Just keep a steady rhythm, and Cooper will take care of the rest."

Her words were meant to reassure me, but they only stirred up nerves as I watched Amy and Belle look like perfect partners, completely in sync.

What was I thinking signing up for this? My first show and I was about to walk into the same ring with riders who made it look like they'd been born in the saddle.

Belle cleared the last line effortlessly, flicking her ears to Amy as she gave her a quick pat on the neck.

Amy walked Belle out of the ring, her face flushed with

pride. She joined us at the rail, Belle's reins draped loosely in one hand. "She's been so good today," Amy said, her voice still buzzing with adrenaline. "I'm thrilled with her."

"She looked amazing," I said honestly. "You two make it look effortless."

Amy waved me off with a sheepish grin. "Trust me, it's not. Belle's a pro, but it took us a while to get here. You'll see —you've got Cooper, and he'll teach you everything you need to know. Just remember to breathe out there."

"And steer," Liz added with a wink. "That's always helpful."

The lightheartedness helped settle my nerves a bit, though I could still feel them humming beneath the surface. "I'll do my best. But honestly, I'm still questioning every decision that led me to this moment. Who gets divorced and decides to take up showing horses in their fifties? Shouldn't I be doing something... safer? Like yoga?"

Amy laughed. "That's what makes it worth it, though. You're brave enough to take on something new. Not everyone can say that."

Liz nodded in agreement. "And after your classes, you can relax and watch the derby. That's always fun to see."

"What's so special about it?" I asked, grateful for the distraction.

"It's a big deal," Liz said, her enthusiasm apparent. "The courses are more technical than a regular hunter course. There are rollbacks, trot fences, and options for which height you want to jump. It really showcases the partnership between horse and rider. Plus, there's prize money, and today's is a qualifier for the regionals."

I glanced back at the hunter ring as the next rider entered. "Sounds intense."

"It is," Liz said, "but it's worth watching. You'll learn a lot."

Amy gave Belle another pat before nodding toward the barn. "I'm going to take her back to her stall. See you guys in a bit?"

Liz pulled what I recognized as the show schedule out of her pocket and looked it over. "I'll head back there with you. I need to make sure the other girls are tacking up. Their classes are next. And Jen, let's get Cooper tacked up in half an hour and get you in the warm-up ring."

My eyes got wide and I gulped but nodded. Liz gave me a wink as she walked away with Amy and Belle.

Where to now, Treat Lady? Ripley asked, his head tilted as he waited for a response. *You're running out of time to catch Miranda's killer if you have to ride in half an hour. And let's be real—once you're in the saddle, your brain's going to short-circuit.*

What are you implying? I asked dryly. Though he wasn't wrong. I was going to be so stressed about riding—there was no way I'd be able to notice anything else once I was on Cooper.

I glanced toward the warm-up ring, where a cluster of riders was schooling their horses. *Let's go back to the warm-up ring. Maybe we'll overhear something… or at least get a feel for what I'm about to walk into.*

~

I MADE my way back to the warm-up ring and leaned against the railing. Ripley sat at my feet, his bright eyes tracking every movement in the ring.

This is a disaster waiting to happen, he observed.

I couldn't help but agree. Warm-up rings were infamous

for being the most stressful part of a horse show. The thought of being out there navigating Cooper through the chaos made me nauseous.

Don't remind me. My grip on Ripley's leash tightened as I tried to calm my nerves.

Miranda appeared beside me so suddenly I nearly jumped. *Relax. You're not in there yet,* she said briskly, her sharp gaze already scanning the ring. *Look at Rachel and Apollo. That's what you should be focusing on. Something's not right with him.*

She pointed to a horse and rider trotting slowly along the rail.

Why? What do you mean? I asked.

Apollo's a top hunter, Miranda said, her eyes narrowing as she watched. *He's supposed to move like a dream—forward, effortless, the kind of horse judges trip over themselves to pin first. But look at him. He's dragging his feet. Rachel knows it.*

I frowned. *How can you tell?*

Miranda gave me a sidelong glance, her tone tinged with impatience. *His entire way of moving, the way she's riding him—all of it. Her legs are busy, seat's tight. She's trying to make him move, but he's not responding. Something's wrong.*

Rachel cast a glance toward the rail, where her trainer stood.

Miranda's attention shifted, her expression darkening. *And there's Victoria. Of course, she's glued to Rachel and Apollo.*

Victoria? I scanned the rail. *The show mom who accused me of eavesdropping?*

Yes. She's by the guy in the white baseball hat, glaring at Rachel like she's willing Apollo to trip over the next jump.

Miranda tilted her head toward another rider circling nearby. *And that's Olivia, Victoria's daughter on the chestnut gelding. Victoria is completely ignoring her.*

I squinted, trying to pick out the rider Miranda mentioned. Olivia was quiet and focused, her horse transitioning seamlessly between gaits. *That's her daughter?*

Yes. And she's a decent rider, too. Olivia's got skill and a good horse, but Victoria can't see it. She's too busy obsessing over Rachel and Apollo. Always has been.

Something about Victoria's focus made me uneasy. She wasn't just watching Rachel, she was fixated. Then, for the briefest moment, her expression softened. A flicker of satisfaction crossed her face.

She seems... pleased, I said hesitantly.

Why wouldn't she be? Miranda's voice dripped with disdain. *Rachel's horse just practically tripped over that jump. He's off, and Victoria's been waiting for this moment. She's always claimed Rachel and Apollo are the only things standing between Olivia and a blue ribbon. But something doesn't sit right.*

What do you mean?

Miranda hesitated, her form flickering slightly. Her mouth opened, then snapped shut, frustration tightening her expression.

Wait, she said, her voice quieter now. *I remember something.*

A pause.

I saw her earlier...

I straightened, my pulse kicking up. *Victoria? Where?*

She was tense. Defensive. We argued. Miranda pressed her fingers to her temples, eyes narrowing in concentration. *I don't remember exactly what she said...*

She exhaled sharply. *But that's all I've got. I know we*

argued. But let's be real—I argued with a lot of people. Doesn't mean they all wanted me dead.

I chewed my lip, trying to piece it all together. Victoria's jealousy was obvious, but Miranda's memories were so fractured. Just flashes of an argument didn't exactly mean murder. And like she said, she argued with people all the time.

Yet, that flicker of satisfaction I'd seen on Victoria's face while she watched Apollo stuck with me.

The loudspeaker crackled, jolting me out of my thoughts.

"Attention, riders! Please remember, you can't buy happiness, but you can buy a fancy horse—and that's practically close enough."

Miranda smirked faintly. *He knows the horse world well.*

Ripley snorted. *So it seems.*

I let out a deep sigh while my thoughts tumbled over each other. Victoria's obsession, Miranda's hazy memory, and Tyler's suspicious history—one of them had to be guilty. Of course, there was no telling how many other people Miranda had antagonized over the years, given her habit of speaking her mind and judging anyone who crossed her path.

I glanced back at the warm-up ring, the chaotic scene mirroring the jumble of questions in my head. And with my own turn in the ring looming, I was running out of time.

Chapter Seven

I headed back toward Cooper's stall, my mind still going over Victoria's strange behavior. The sound of voices drew my attention.

A man stood near a row of stalls, his posture relaxed but confident.

"Don't worry about a thing," he said, his smooth voice carrying easily. "He'll be perfect for your class."

Recognition clicked. Tyler. The trainer Amy had pointed out earlier.

I slowed my steps, straining to hear more.

"Are you sure?" A woman's voice, anxious and hopeful. "He's been so spooky lately..."

"Trust me. By the time you get on, he'll be the picture-perfect hunter horse, exactly what the judges want."

My stomach twisted. The rumors about Tyler's methods and how his riders always win surfaced in my mind.

Miranda materialized beside me, her form flickering with agitation. *That snake,* she hissed. *I remember now. I caught him with those bottles—those "calming supplements" he claimed were natural.*

What happened? I asked silently.

I confronted him. Told him I'd expose what he was doing to those horses. It wasn't just about cheating anymore—it was abuse. Drugging horses to make them manageable, risking their health just so his clients could win ribbons.

Miranda's form wavered, her voice tight with anger. *I always thought he was ambitious, but not... ruthless. I guess you never know what people are capable of.*

I pressed myself against the wall as Tyler and his client walked past, neither noticing me in the shadows. Tyler's easy smile and confident stride showed no hint of the darkness Miranda had described, but her words echoed in my head. What else was he capable of if his reputation had been threatened?

I continued toward Cooper's stall, my mind churning over what I'd overheard. The familiar scent of hay and horses filled my nose as I walked down the aisle.

Cooper's white face appeared over his stall door, ears pricked forward. *You look troubled.*

Just thinking. I dug in my pocket for the peppermint I'd stashed earlier. *That trainer, Tyler Collins, was just talking about making someone's horse calm for their class, but Miranda said he was drugging the horses in a way that risks their health. She even said she confronted him about it.*

Cooper gently accepted the treat, savoring each bite. *And so I assume you're questioning if what she said is true? Or if she's overreacting?*

Well, do trainers do that? I asked, leaning against his door. *Is it normal to give horses things to make them calm? I mean, I get it. No one wants to get hurt, and horses can be unpredictable. No offense, but even you have your moments.*

Ripley sat at my feet, ears perked and head tilted. *Excuse me, Treat Lady, I saw that treat you handed him.*

Where's mine? I've been working even harder than Cooper today. All he's done is lounge in here and eat.

I rolled my eyes and reached into my other pocket, pulling out a dog treat I'd stashed earlier. *Fine, here. Hardest-working detective on four legs, I swear.*

Ripley snatched it eagerly, crunching it down with a smug tilt of his head. *It's not bragging if it's true.*

Cooper gave a low nicker, clearly amused. *Back to the topic at hand, there's a difference between supplements and sedatives,* he pointed out. *One helps. The other masks.*

Miranda appeared, arms crossed. *Stop making excuses for him. You know it's wrong.*

Do I? I turned to face her. *I've only been in this sport for barely two years, and the show world is entirely new to me. Maybe this is one of those things everyone knows about but doesn't discuss. Like how nobody talks about how much everything costs.*

Trust your instincts, Cooper nudged my shoulder. *You knew something was wrong when you heard him. That's why you stopped to listen.*

He was right. Whatever Tyler was doing, the secrecy around it spoke volumes. If it was completely innocent, why the hushed conversations? And why had Miranda confronted him about it?

So what do we do about it? I asked, looking between Cooper and Miranda. *I can't exactly march up to Detective Hayes and tell him Miranda's ghost told me Tyler was drugging horses and she confronted him about it.*

We need proof, Miranda's form flickered with frustration. *Physical evidence.*

I pressed my lips together, resisting the urge to argue. And how exactly was I supposed to find that?

Ripley's head snapped up, nose twitching. *Speaking of evidence...* He trotted toward the end of the stalls, leash dragging behind him, stopping to look back at me expectantly. *That shiny guy is coming this way! And he's carrying something...*

I followed Ripley, trying to look casual as I pretended to check my phone. At the end of the aisle, I spotted Tyler walking quickly toward the parking lot, a small black duffel bag clutched in his hand.

Miranda appeared beside me. *I bet that's his supply bag. If you could get a look inside—*

I watched Tyler weave through the vehicles before stopping at a truck, tossing the bag in, and then turning back toward the show office. I noted which truck was his—a sleek black pickup with custom wheels—and then stepped back towards the stalls to avoid him seeing me.

Good, Miranda nodded. *Now we know where to look.*

We're not breaking into his truck, I hissed.

Of course not, Ripley huffed. *But maybe we should take a walk past it. My nose is excellent at detecting interesting smells, as you well know.*

I glanced at my watch. I needed to get moving. I had to get Cooper tacked up soon, but there was still time for a casual stroll through the parking lot with my dog.

Just remember, Cooper cautioned, *whatever you find, be careful. It seems Tyler has a lot more to lose than just some ribbons.*

~

THE PARKING LOT stretched out behind the showgrounds, a maze of trucks and trailers baking in the sun.

"Ready for a walk, Ripley?"

He leaped forward, his little legs flying. *Finally. My detective skills have been going to waste.*

We stepped out of the stable area into the sunlight. I pulled out my phone, pretending to check messages while we meandered between the vehicles, trying to look casual. A few people nodded as they passed, but most rushed by without a glance.

We approached Tyler's truck from the passenger side. Ripley's nose twitched as he sniffed along the running board.

Same smell, he confirmed. *Like Miranda's thermos, but stronger.*

Miranda materialized next to the truck. *Look through the window. The bag is right there on the front seat.*

I can't exactly peek in without looking suspicious, I muttered.

Of course you can—just make it quick, Miranda insisted with an exasperated wave of her transparent hand.

I looked around, and seeing the coast clear, I climbed up the running board and looked in the window. The duffel bag sat open on the front seat, the zipper partially undone. I leaned closer, catching a glimpse of a small plastic syringe and a vial of amber liquid labeled acepromazine. My breath caught. This had to be it—the proof Miranda was talking about.

Miranda appeared beside me, her arms crossed. *There it is. I knew it. He's drugging his horses.*

I moved away from the window, my mind racing. Though I was no expert on equine medications, I figured Miranda knew what she was talking about. After all, she'd been a successful trainer for decades, and if anyone could spot something suspicious, it would be her.

The discovery of that vial was exactly the kind of

evidence we needed, but it also meant that Tyler was willing to do whatever it took to win, even if it meant drugging horses.

I felt nauseous just thinking about it. As an amateur rider still learning the ropes, I'd always assumed the competitive spirit at shows was intense but ethical. Now I was seeing a darker side of the sport—one where ribbons and reputation apparently meant more than the welfare of these amazing animals. The fact that someone would deliberately sedate these horses, potentially putting both animals and riders at risk, made my blood boil.

The crunch of gravel made me straighten up. Tyler was walking back toward his truck, his expression dark as he talked on his phone.

"Time to go," I whispered to Ripley. We turned and walked casually away, but not before I caught a snippet of Tyler's conversation.

"Don't worry about it," he said, his voice low and firm. "Everything's handled."

~

I STARTED TO WALK AWAY, but Miranda's ghost was practically vibrating with indignation.

Are you really just going to let him get away with this? Miranda demanded. *After what we just saw?*

Maybe we should take a breath and think this through... Just go tell the detective what you found, Jen... Cooper's sage advice drifted in my mind.

Think it through? Tell the detective about another of her hunches? Miranda snapped. *He's got drugs in his truck! Someone needs to stand up to him NOW!*

Maybe not the nervous amateur rider who knows

nothing about horse showing? Ripley's mental eye-roll was practically audible.

Well, excuse me for caring about the horses! Miranda huffed.

My temples throbbed. My palms were sweating. *All of you, please—*

I didn't know what to do. Miranda was sure Tyler was drugging his horses, which meant there was a good chance he wanted to keep her quiet... And he was acting so shady... But I couldn't very well drag Detective Hayes to his truck!

Someone has to DO something! Miranda screeched. *These show circuit pretty boys think they can—*

Between finding Miranda's body, having her ghost back-seat-driving every decision, AND now finding suspicious drugs in Tyler's truck, something in me snapped.

Before I knew what I was doing, I had turned around and called out, "Tyler?"

He glanced up from his phone and looked at me, confusion in his eyes. "Yes?"

"The acepromazine. I saw it." My voice squeaked as I said the words. Ugh, so not the best way to start the conversation. "Miranda told me—I mean, I heard about you drugging horses before shows."

Tyler's face morphed into a patronizing smile as his gaze swept over me.

"I don't know what you think you saw or what you heard, but everything I use is legal and properly prescribed."

Miranda floated through him repeatedly. *He's lying! Well, okay, maybe not technically lying, but he's definitely being sketchy!*

"But Miranda said—" My voice cracked like a teenage boy's.

"Miranda," Tyler cut me off with a shake of his head,

"was always making accusations without understanding modern training methods. I'm sorry about what happened to her, and if you were friends or one of her students, I'm sorry for your loss, but her accusations about me were uncalled for. We use legitimate supplements and medications to keep our horses healthy and competing at their best. And how long have you been in the horse business...?"

Heat crept into my face as my stomach did a particularly awful flip. I'd never felt more like an outsider.

Okay, this is getting awkward... Ripley shuffled his paws. *Maybe we should go back to Cooper.*

Don't let him intimidate you! Miranda fumed. *These arrogant young trainers think they own the sport!*

My hands wouldn't stop shaking.

"I just thought..."

"You thought you'd accuse a professional trainer of drugging horses based on rumors?" Tyler shook his head, his expression suggesting he was dealing with a particularly dim child. "If you'll excuse me, I have clients waiting."

He strode away, leaving me feeling about two inches tall. My legs felt like jelly, and I was pretty sure my face was roughly the color of a stop sign.

Well, that could have gone better. Though I still say we should follow him. Miranda huffed.

Ripley sighed. *I tried to tell you both this was a bad idea. But does anyone listen to the dog? Nooo...*

Chapter Eight

I stood in Cooper's stall, brush trembling in my hand as I tried to focus on his white coat. My face burned with embarrassment from the confrontation with Tyler.

Steady. Left side first. Focus on the brush, not Tyler. Cooper's gentle thoughts washed over me.

"I can't believe I made such a fool of myself," I muttered, attacking a manure stain with more vigor than necessary.

Miranda materialized through the stall wall. *That ARROGANT pretty boy! The way he sweet-talks his clients about his 'methods'...*

Are you sure he did it? Ripley asked. *Slicked-back hair or not, he doesn't really seem like a killer.*

Who else would want to kill me? Miranda screeched. *I know I wasn't everyone's cup of tea—because heaven forbid people actually do the work. But Tyler? He's the only one I've called out recently. I just could not tolerate another show of him skirting the rules to make his horses easy for his weekend warrior amateurs.*

Speaking of laziness, Jennifer, Miranda's eyes bore into

me, *are you putting ANY effort into cleaning those stains? Show some respect for your horse!*

Ouch! Ripley's eyes grew even bigger than usual.

Miranda huffed.

Now, now, Cooper interjected, *that's uncalled for. Jen always looks after me and ensures I shine like the star that I am.*

Just then, Amy appeared at the stall door, interrupting Miranda's tirade, her usual infectious grin lighting up her face.

"Hey, Jen! It's almost time!" she chirped, her voice a welcome distraction from Miranda's relentless criticism. "Liz sent me to help you out. She wants you tacked up so you have plenty of time to warm up." Amy's presence was like a breath of fresh air, and I couldn't help but feel a little relieved. Finally, a reprieve from the Miranda madness.

I reached for Cooper's saddle pad, trying to push thoughts of Tyler aside.

We can't just let him get away with this! Miranda continued as she paced.

Amy chatted about her rounds while helping me tack up, completely oblivious to Miranda hovering nearby.

Sharp blue eyes tracked my every movement as I fumbled with Cooper's girth. *For heaven's sake, you're going to make it too loose,* Miranda snapped. *And your saddle pad is crooked. How do you expect to ride properly when you can't even manage basic tack?* She drifted closer, her silver ponytail swishing as she circled me.

I gritted my teeth and adjusted the pad, trying to focus on Amy's cheerful rundown of the show while Miranda continued her dual critique of my horsemanship and Tyler's training methods.

Cooper, at least, seemed amused by the whole situation, his thoughts reaching me with a dry, *Well, she's not wrong about the saddle pad.*

I continued to fumble with Cooper's girth, my hands still shaking. *I can't do this. I'm not a detective—I'm barely even a rider. I can't even tack you up properly. I tried confronting Tyler and made a complete fool of myself. What am I even doing here?*

Oh, don't be ridiculous, Miranda huffed, floating through the stall door. *You're jumping two feet, and your horse could do the courses blindfolded. Trust me, you'll be no worse than half of the two-foot riders here. It boggles my mind that there is even a two-foot division, but I digress... We need to focus on Tyler. You need to—"*

Gee, thanks. I feel so much better.

Jen, let's focus on our rounds for now, Cooper interrupted, his voice calm but firm. *Yes, I have done just a few of these rounds before,* he added with a chuckle, *but it's a team sport, and we're in this together. One thing at a time. You've done all you can for Miranda for now, let's focus on your show now.*

Cooper has a point, Ripley piped in. *And hey, worst case? Weird-Dead Lady gets to haunt Tyler forever. Win-win.*

Miranda's form wavered. *Thanks for the support, the lot of you. Fine. I'll go investigate myself.* Miranda disappeared with a theatrical huff.

I took a deep breath. They were right. It was time to focus on what I came here for—riding in my first horse show.

"Amy, would you mind helping me with Cooper's bridle? I need to grab my show jacket from Liz's truck."

"Of course!" Amy reached for the bridle while I gathered my scattered nerves. Between Miranda's murder, Tyler's suspicious behavior, and my first show, I felt pulled in too many directions. But Cooper was waiting, steady as ever, reminding me what mattered right now.

≈

JEN! That smell again—from the thermos and Tyler's truck! Ripley yanked hard on his leash, nearly pulling my arm out of its socket.

I planted my feet, trying to resist Ripley's determined pull. "Ripley, no!" I hissed. "I'm done playing detective."

Same smell. Same as Weird-Dead Lady's thermos. Ripley's thoughts burst into my mind.

Miranda materialized in a flash. *Someone MURDERED me, Jennifer!*

"I'm sorry, but no. Absolutely not. I have a class in—" I checked my phone, "less than forty minutes. I need to focus on not falling off Cooper in front of everyone."

But the smell! Ripley's thoughts were insistent. *Bad smell. Same bad smell.*

Miranda drifted alongside me, flickering with irritation. *Jennifer, this could be crucial evidence. Are you really going to ignore it?*

Yes, actually, I am. I crossed my arms. *I found your thermos. I handed it to Detective Hayes. I confronted Tyler. Case closed. I am officially retiring from my Nancy Drew phase.*

Cooper's thoughts drifted from his stall. *You could at least look. I'm not going anywhere.*

You too, Cooper? I threw my hands up. *Seriously?* Ripley and Miranda just stared at me. Cooper was silent. *Fine. FINE! But this is the last time.*

I let Ripley lead me down the aisle. Each step felt like a

betrayal of my promise to focus on showing. Other riders bustled past, absorbed in their own pre-ride routines. At least they weren't questioning why the middle-aged amateur was being dragged down the aisle by a Boston Terrier.

Ripley veered left, dragging me past a row of stalls. I sighed but let him pull me along.

Left here, Ripley directed, pulling me closer. *It's stronger.*

I can't believe I'm doing this. I should be memorizing my course.

Miranda sailed ahead of us. *Oh, stop complaining. You weren't going to remember it anyway.*

Thanks for the vote of confidence. She probably wasn't wrong, though.

Ripley slowed in front of a stall, nose working furiously. Then I saw it—a laminated stall card stapled neatly to the door.

It said Apollo.

I blinked. Apollo? As in Rachel and Apollo? The horse that Miranda said didn't look right?

I followed Ripley into the stall, watching as he sniffed determinedly and made his way by a feed bucket.

I knelt down, pushing aside some shavings where he was snorting dramatically. A glint of plastic caught my eye —an empty syringe. When my fingers brushed it, an overwhelming feeling of cold, grim determination washed over me.

I dropped the syringe, gasping. *But this is Apollo's stall. Apollo isn't even Tyler's horse—why would he drug him?*

Maybe he's branching out? Ripley suggested. *Expanding his criminal enterprise?*

Miranda hovered nearby, her form flickering with agitation. *Let's think it through. If someone is drugging Apollo, who benefits if he performs poorly?*

Well, Tyler's students would have a better chance at winning, but so would plenty of others... I shook my head. Plus, Tyler came across so confident and smug. This felt different.

And how does my coffee fit in? Miranda pressed. *Was I drugged to keep me quiet about the horse doping?*

My mind raced. Was Tyler trying to sabotage Rachel and Apollo? Did that actually happen at horse shows? Were people really that intense even at local shows? And did Miranda confront him about it, and he killed her for it?

I thought back to the gossip I'd heard throughout the day about Tyler.

Miranda's form crackled with frustration. *CLEARLY, something is not right here.*

Hey, at least this time you have something real to show Hayes, Ripley offered.

Either way, quit dithering around, and perhaps we could DO something with this? You're the one who keeps saying you have classes to do, so let's move it.

I stared at the syringe. Another piece of the puzzle. Maybe Hayes would take me seriously this time.

I sighed. Just when I thought I was done investigating. How was I ever going to be ready to ride?

The announcer's voice crackled over the loudspeaker. "Remember, folks, ambition is great, but there's no ribbon worth compromising your integrity for. Or as my dear old mama used to say—climb that ladder to success carefully. The higher you go, the harder you fall."

❧

I FOUND Detective Hayes near the show office. For a moment, I just stood there, the syringe feeling like it weighed a ton in my hand. I took a deep breath as I approached. Here I was yet again attempting to give him evidence that I had no way to prove had any relevance, but what else could I do?

He noticed me hovering and raised an eyebrow.

"Detective Hayes? Do you have a minute? I, um... I found something else... And there's something I need to tell you about."

I thought I saw a flash of annoyance across his face, but he nodded and gestured me to follow him.

"I found this in Apollo's stall," I said when we stopped, my hands shaking as I held up the syringe. "And there's something else—Tyler Collins... well, I've been hearing things about him drugging horses. Miranda was going to expose him for it. I even confronted him about it, but he denied everything."

Hayes sighed, rubbing his temple. "Look, Ms. Harlow, I appreciate your concern, but we don't even know if her death was anything but natural causes. And finding an empty syringe proves nothing. I'm sure many horses get medications by syringe here. And rumors about arguments? That's not evidence."

How could I explain any of what I knew without sounding completely unhinged?

"Look, Ms. Harlow," Hayes said with practiced patience, "I appreciate you bringing these things to my attention, but unless you have something concrete, there's nothing more I can do."

I opened my mouth to argue, then closed it again. No, I had to try harder. Miranda was murdered.

"But Miranda had confronted Tyler about drugging

horses. She thought he was abusing them, cutting corners... then suddenly she's dead? And now there's this syringe in Apollo's stall..."

I trailed off, seeing his expression. "I know it's all circumstantial, but surely it's worth looking into?"

Hayes shook his head. "Ms. Harlow, I get that something feels off to you, but I can't launch a murder investigation based on rumors and hunches."

"But the coffee—" I stopped myself. What was I supposed to say? That my dog confirmed it smelled like the drugs Tyler used on his horses? That Miranda's ghost told me she'd been murdered? That I had a psychic vision when I touched the syringe?

Finally, I managed a weak "Thank you for your time" and turned away, my cheeks burning.

Miranda materialized beside me, crackling with fury. *That's IT? You're just giving up? Do you even REALIZE what this means?* Her form flickered violently.

I'll be trapped here FOREVER while my killer walks free! You HAVE to tell him about your visions. About me! About ALL of it!

"I can't," I whispered. "Who's going to believe I can see ghosts and talk to animals? Everyone will think I'm crazy."

So that's it then? Miranda's voice rose, though only I could hear it. *I'm supposed to spend ETERNITY haunting horse shows while my murderer gets away with it? Because you're too worried about what people will think of you?*

I felt her disappointment like a physical thing. *I'm sorry. But I have to think about myself for once. I came here to do something that terrifies me—to prove to myself I could. And right now, that's all I can handle.*

Miranda's presence grew distant, leaving behind a bone-deep chill and the knowledge that without my help, her death would surely be written off as natural causes.

But I had to focus on what I came here for—my first horse show. I'd done everything I could. Now it was time to do something for myself.

I squared my shoulders and made my way back to Cooper's stall.

Chapter Nine

"There you are!" Amy rounded the corner, my show jacket draped over her arm. "I got worried when you didn't come back from the trailer."

I forced myself to focus on her words, trying to push away the memory of Detective Hayes' dismissive tone. Right now, showing was all that mattered. Or at least, that's what I kept telling myself.

Amy nodded knowingly. "Been there. Thought you might be hiding in the trailer having second thoughts. Come on, let's get you ready. At least Cooper's been patiently waiting with his tack on—thank goodness for the delay in the hunter ring."

My stomach lurched as I thought about what was ahead. Different nerves now, at least. Show nerves seemed almost quaint compared to what I'd been dealing with.

Amy helped me into my jacket while I tried to concentrate on the familiar routine. Hairnet on. Helmet on. Breathe. The mundane tasks helped while my mind tried to settle.

Cooper's head appeared over the stall door. *You know what helps with nerves? Cookies.*

I gave him a weak smile, grateful for the distraction.

Cookies help with everything, Ripley agreed.

Yes, I'm wise. And hungry.

You're always hungry.

Cooper managed to look dignified despite the accusation. *You say that like it's a bad thing.*

I reached out to scratch Cooper's nose, feeling the comforting roughness of his coat under my fingers while Amy fussed with my collar. I was grateful for Cooper's steady presence, Amy's unwavering support, and Ripley's boundless energy.

Miranda materialized beside me, arms crossed, watching but saying nothing. Her silence spoke volumes.

"Ready?" Amy asked, brushing invisible lint from my shoulder.

No. Not even close. But I nodded anyway. Time to be just another nervous amateur at her first show. Nothing more.

~

I GUIDED Cooper into the warm-up ring, trying to ignore the sea of perfect-looking equestrians circling around us. A willowy teen cantered past on a gleaming bay, her position flawless, her boots spotless.

I glanced down at my own boots—budget-friendly ones I'd bought for the show, feeling proud at the time, like a *real* equestrian. Normally, I rode in paddock boots and half chaps, which actually fit my not-so-tall, not-so-willowy frame. Even the attire wasn't made for people like me.

Stop comparing yourself to the teenagers, Cooper's voice

cut through my spiral of self-doubt. *They're basically spring-loaded at that age. You have life experience.*

And better snacks, Ripley added from his spot beside Amy at the rail.

Miranda's ghost materialized nearby, arms crossed. *Since you've decided to abandon our investigation, I suppose I should at least make sure you don't embarrass yourself.* She looked me and Cooper over. *Your reins are uneven. And you didn't get that manure stain off.*

I grimaced and adjusted my reins. At least she was speaking to me, even though just seeing her reminded me how much I'd failed her.

"Focus, Jen. Heels down, shoulders back," Liz's voice called out from the center of the arena. "You know the drill," she continued. "Don't worry about anyone else, just you and Cooper." Her voice carried the familiar mix of encouragement and challenge that had gotten me through two years of lessons.

I gathered my reins and took a deep breath, trying to remember everything she had taught me. Heels down. Hands quiet. Look ahead. Don't collapse at the waist.

"Good. Now let's work on those transitions. Start with a trot, and then when you're ready, ask for a canter."

True to his steady, schoolmaster self, as soon as I asked, Cooper picked up a steady trot, his rhythm helping calm my nerves.

"Don't think too much," Amy shouted encouragingly. "You know what to do! Believe in yourself!"

Miranda sniffed. *You look stiff as a board. Loosen up before Cooper starts looking like you.*

Ignore the peanut gallery, otherwise known as Miranda, Cooper advised. *We've got this.*

"Okay, once you've done a couple of canter laps, you can

pop over this cross-rail," Liz called, gesturing to the small jump she was standing next to.

My stomach clenched. The tiny practice jump looked enormous.

Oh for heaven's sake, Miranda huffed, floating closer. *If your coach said you're ready to show, you better at least be able to handle a cross-rail in the warm-up ring.*

She really had no clue what it was like to learn to ride as an adult, did she?

She's right, you know, Cooper chimed in. *Cross-rails are easy-peasy. And I'd have bucked you off already if I didn't think you could handle it.*

Gee, thanks, I guess.

Cooper chuckled in my head.

I took a deep breath and turned Cooper toward the jump.

~

"READY?" Amy asked with a big grin.

"Ready as I'll ever be," I said, giving her what I hoped was a grin, though I'm sure it looked more like a deer in headlights.

"You've got this," Liz patted me on my thigh and led me to the in-gate. "Remember to breathe."

My legs felt weak as I stepped into the hunter ring, and my hands shook. How I was going to remember the course, never mind stay on the back of Cooper over jumps while feeling like a wet noodle, I had no idea, but it was time.

And the jumps looked enormous, even though I knew they were only two feet high. What on earth was I thinking?

We've got this, Cooper assured me. *And you've got peppermints in your pocket, so my motivation is high.*

I heard my name called over the speakers—"This is number 132, Jennifer Harlow, riding Cooper's Silver Linings."

Wow, this really was happening.

I picked up the trot, trying to focus on the course I'd attempted to memorize. My brain farted, and I completely forgot where my first jump was. My heart leaped into my throat.

Seriously, you've forgotten your first jump already? This should go well. Miranda appeared alongside the rail, arms crossed as per usual. *It's that diagonal with yellow flowers at the top of the ring.*

Ah right. Okay. First jump on the diagonal, then the judge's line, followed by another diagonal to the outside line, finishing with a single diagonal. Simple enough in theory, but my brain didn't agree.

You don't need to recite it, Cooper advised. *I know where we're going. They're always a similar pattern, and I've been watching the others while you've been panicking.*

All right, here we go. We picked up the canter and headed down the long side. I attempted to remember everything Liz had drilled into me.

Less thinking, more feeling, Cooper suggested as we approached the first fence. He gathered himself underneath me and easily popped over it. Despite the small size of the jump, my legs slipped behind me, and I landed heavily on his neck on the landing. Cooper grunted in response.

Ugh. *I'm sorry, Cooper!* My nerves were getting the best of me.

Keep your heels down and legs under you! Miranda yelled from the rail. *And for heaven's sake, use your core! Your horse shouldn't have to do all the work out there!*

I was thankful I was the only one who could hear her—I

knew she was right. It was embarrassing enough just hearing her in my head.

The judge's line loomed ahead—two jumps set, in theory, six strides apart. Cooper tried to adjust his stride to get the right distance, but I held the reins too tight, letting my fear take over and holding him back.

Loosen those reins, he huffed. *I can't get the striding with you holding my face like that. Trust me, I know what I'm doing here.*

My death grip cost us our distance, and we got seven strides instead of six between the jumps. To be fair, I didn't really care about the perfect distance, I was just happy we'd now gotten through three jumps. Horrible equitation aside, I was still on his back, which counted for something.

I could practically hear Miranda rolling her eyes.

The diagonal line came next, followed—more quickly than it should have because of my bad steering—by the outside line. Cooper took care of the distances despite me while I did my best to focus on staying with his motion and not interfering. He was a pro at this, and I was definitely being more of a passenger than a pilot, but at least I remembered where we were going.

Give me more rein, Cooper suggested again as we approached the last line. *These jumps are speed bumps, but I still would like my face.*

The final jump approached. One last effort and we were over, this time landing together, like I might actually kind of know what I was doing.

And now the courtesy circle, Cooper reminded me as I started to relax too soon. *Try to look elegant for at least ten more seconds.*

I brought him back to a trot, completing our circle

before walking out of the ring. My hands shook as I patted his neck.

"Good job!" Liz smiled, meeting us at the gate. "Work on making wider turns for the next rounds and keeping your heels down over the jumps, but you're doing great."

I nodded, still trembling. I knew she was being too kind, but I was still proud we'd completed the course. Two more rounds to go, plus a flat class. A hot flash kicked in at the thought of going back in the ring.

You didn't fall off, Cooper offered helpfully. *That's always a win in my book. Though next time, maybe try actually letting me go to the jumps? Just a suggestion.*

I shifted in the saddle, my legs still quivering as I reached down to stroke Cooper's neck in appreciation. Thanks to him, we'd survived our first course, despite how messy it looked. Eight jumps down, sixteen more to go. Hopefully, I'd be in the saddle for all of them.

Amy came bouncing over with Ripley tugging at his leash. "You did it! And you remembered the course!"

I laughed. "Yes, the bar is set low enough that I've accomplished my goal for the day."

Amy rolled her eyes and swatted my leg. "Ugh, you. Give yourself more credit. What you've done is amazing and so awesome. Learning to ride as an adult and then show? You're a rock star."

Jeez, don't let it go to your head, Ripley commented, sitting at my feet and looking up at me with his signature head tilt. *You're just sitting on the back of a big, comfy couch, aren't you? I will say it was interesting to watch, anyway. I particularly enjoyed that landing after jump one where you ended up on Cooper's neck. Very creative.*

Thanks for the support. I gave him a side eye.

Hey, you stayed on, that's what matters! Though maybe

next time try using those leg things attached to your body? Just a suggestion from someone who walks on four legs naturally.

"You're going to be fine for the next rounds," Amy assured me, completely oblivious to my conversation with the peanut gallery. "First-round nerves are always the worst. Now you can just focus on having fun!"

Fun might be a stretch, Cooper chimed in. *But at least you know I won't let you fall off. Or I'll do my best anyway. And Ripley, I don't appreciate being called a couch.*

Ripley tilted his head and gazed at him, unperturbed.

I patted Cooper's neck again, grateful for his steady presence despite his occasional sass. Between my four-legged comedian, my ghostly critic, and my very human cheerleaders, I had quite the support team. Even if half of them couldn't resist giving me grief. But what are friends for?

Chapter Ten

"**G**reat job!" Liz called, patting me on the leg as I came out of the ring. "And look at you, even a ribbon in the flat class!"

I laughed as I swung my leg over Cooper's back and slid to the ground, my knees nearly buckling on impact. Liz steadied me and gave me a big hug. "I'm so proud of you!" she said, her eyes shining with uncharacteristic tears.

My legs wobbled, my hands trembled, but underneath it all, a warmth spread through me. I'd actually done it. I'd competed in my first horse show—as a newbie rider, at age 51. I even had a crisp green sixth-place ribbon from the flat class to show for it. Take that, children in bows. Yes, I was being petty, but I deserved to be after the day I'd had.

"Thank you so much, Liz," I said, squeezing her back. I let her go and stepped back, looking her in the eyes. "I can hardly believe it. I don't know where I would be if I hadn't walked into your barn two years ago. And Cooper. Wow, I'm just so thankful for him. He's amazing." Liz gave me another tearful smile as I turned and gave Cooper his own hug.

Amy jogged up beside me, Ripley's leash in hand.

"You did it!" Amy squealed. "I knew you could do it!" She wrapped her arms around me and gave me a big squeeze. "And isn't Cooper just the best?" she continued, giving him a big pat on the neck. "You are such a good boy, Coop!"

I could feel the warmth of appreciation radiating from him as he turned to nuzzle Amy.

"Alright, warm fuzzies over," Liz said, shifting back into coach mode. "Go get Cooper untacked, and then let's watch the derby together."

"Yes!" Amy said excitedly. "The derbies are amazing to watch. Some of the riders make it look like they're doing nothing while their horses do these amazing turns and huge jumps. They make it look so easy!"

"As long as I'm watching from the ground," I laughed. "My heart can only take so much excitement in one day."

~

AFTER UNTACKING Cooper and lavishing him with treats for putting up with me all day, I headed to the trailer to change. I could feel my body stiffening up now that the adrenaline was wearing off. Who knew three rounds of jumping and a flat class could make parts hurt that I didn't even know existed? I was definitely going to feel this tomorrow.

Ripley padded along beside me, seeming content after his day of showground adventures. But as we passed a row of stalls, he suddenly stiffened. His nose twitched frantically, and before I could brace myself, he yanked hard on his leash, nearly pulling me off balance.

Jen! That smell—something's happening RIGHT NOW!

I stumbled, barely catching myself.

You've got to be kidding me. AGAIN?

Ripley pulled, insistent.

I squeezed my eyes shut, fighting the urge to pretend I hadn't heard him. I'd already done my good deed for the day, hadn't I? My entire body had earned a break.

But deep down, I knew I wouldn't ignore him.

Okay, okay, I'm coming! Just stop making it so obvious.

He slowed down a fraction, and I let him guide me closer, trying to appear casual.

Up ahead, the smell is in that same place again!

Ripley pulled me forward, and as we got closer, my stomach dropped. He was leading me to Apollo's stall. Again.

I slowed him down so I could peek through the metal bars without being seen.

I caught a flash of movement. Someone stood by Apollo's feed bucket, their back partially turned, a syringe in their hand. I watched as they squeezed something into Apollo's feed.

The figure shifted, and I caught a glimpse of their face.

It was Victoria!

Chaos erupted all at once. Ripley barked sharply, making Victoria jump and spin around. Apollo's head shot up from his feed bucket with a startled snort that set off a chain reaction of whinnies down the barn aisle. Even Cooper, back in his stall, joined the equine chorus.

Victoria's face went chalk-white when she saw me. The syringe fell to the ground as she tried to bolt, but in her panic, she caught her feet in Ripley's leash and went sprawling.

She scrambled up, her perfect show-mom composure shattered. "This isn't what it looks like," she snapped, backing away. "I'm checking on Apollo for Rachel."

"With a syringe?" I asked.

Victoria flinched. "What are you even doing here?" Her voice rose sharply. "Are you following me?"

I stepped forward, blocking her escape route. "I just saw you putting something in Apollo's feed."

"Supplements. He needs his supplements," she stammered, her eyes darting around the stall. "Rachel asked me to—"

"No, she didn't." The certainty in my voice surprised even me.

Oh God. Miranda appeared suddenly, her form snapping into place beside me. *I remember now! I caught her this morning during my barn check. She was in Apollo's stall, fumbling with something, and when I confronted her, she started babbling excuses. But I knew she was lying.*

Her fists clenched, the rest of the memory surging through her. *I told her I was going to the show steward. I said they'd want to know why she was sneaking around another competitor's horse.*

Miranda turned to me, eyes blazing. *That's it. That's why she—* She broke off, her form flickering with rage. *She couldn't let me report her.*

The pieces slammed into place. The syringe. Apollo. The coffee.

Victoria had done it. She poisoned Miranda.

"Miranda caught you in here this morning, didn't she?" I said. "And you had to stop her from going to the show steward."

Victoria's face drained of color. "How... how could you possibly know that? Nobody was there. Nobody saw us."

Her breath hitched, her gaze darting toward the stall aisle before snapping back to me. "Did someone tell you? Who have you been talking to?"

She took a sharp step toward me, her expression shifting from panic to something colder. My pulse spiked.

"Someone help!" I shouted. "Detective Hayes!" I yelled. It was a long shot, but maybe he was still around.

Victoria lunged forward suddenly, shoving me hard against the stall door. Apollo snorted and danced in his stall. Nearby horses whinnied and squealed in response.

Ripley let out a sharp bark and sprang forward, teeth bared. Victoria shrieked and stumbled back, kicking at him. "Get that dog away from me!"

He held his ground, growling. *I can bite her any time, Jen. Just say the word.*

"You can't prove anything," Victoria hissed. "It's your word against mine, and who are you? Some middle-aged rookie who doesn't even belong here? Nobody will believe you."

I swallowed hard, my heart hammering. She might be right. I had no actual proof, and I wasn't exactly an expert at this whole detective thing. But I'd seen what I'd seen. And I wasn't the only one.

"You might be right about all that," I admitted, "but Miranda told me what happened."

Victoria froze. "Excuse me?"

"She remembered catching you in here this morning. She remembered what you did."

Her eyes darted wildly around the stall. "That's impossible," she snapped. "Miranda's dead."

"And yet, here we are."

Footsteps pounded down the aisle. Detective Hayes appeared, taking in the scene.

Victoria spun toward him, tears welling up. "This woman assaulted me! She's been harassing me all day, and now she's making wild accusations—"

"I just caught her trying to drug Apollo," I cut in. "And she poisoned Miranda's coffee."

"I did not!" Victoria shrieked. She pressed her hands to her face, smudging her flawless makeup.

"I didn't—" Victoria's voice cracked as she continued. "I didn't mean to kill her. The coffee was just supposed to make her sick enough to leave before she could report anything. It wasn't supposed to..."

She let out a ragged breath, fingers trembling as they wiped at her damp cheeks. "My daughter works so hard, but she's never going to beat Rachel and Apollo. I just... I just wanted to give her a chance. Just for this one important class..."

"By poisoning a horse and a woman? That's your idea of leveling the playing field?" Hayes let out a short, humorless laugh and shook his head. He stepped forward, his expression grim. "You have the right to remain silent. Anything you say can and will be used against you in a court of law..."

As Detective Hayes continued reading her rights, Victoria seemed to collapse in on herself, all the fight draining away. She kept mumbling "Olivia... my poor Olivia..." as Hayes led her away, her perfect show-mom facade completely shattered.

I stood there watching Hayes lead Victoria away, my mind reeling. A woman had died all because another mother was so desperate to see her daughter win that she'd lost sight of everything else. The thought of Olivia finding out what her mother had done made me want to be sick. Yet again. My poor stomach had had a day.

Some people forget it's supposed to be about the horses, Cooper's voice drifted softly from his stall, wise as always.

Ripley pressed against my leg. *You okay, Jen?*

I wasn't sure how to answer that. In one day, I'd completed my first horse show, helped solve a murder, and discovered that the competitive drive that made this sport so thrilling could also turn deadly toxic.

Hayes turned back before leading Victoria around the corner. "You know," he called, his expression thoughtful, "you've got good instincts. Most people wouldn't have pieced this together."

I fought the urge to laugh hysterically. Good instincts? If he only knew my "detective team" consisted of a bossy ghost, a wise-cracking dog with a nose for trouble, and a horse who thought he was a philosophy professor. But I just nodded, not quite trusting myself to speak.

"Thanks for your help," he continued. "Maybe I'll call you in on my next case." He winked, squared his shoulders, and nudged Victoria forward.

Great. Now the detective thought I was some kind of amateur sleuth. Next thing I knew, Ripley would be demanding a trench coat and tiny magnifying glass.

Then again, after today? Maybe it wasn't that ridiculous after all.

Chapter Eleven

I found Cooper dozing in his stall, one hip cocked, looking entirely unbothered by the fact we'd just helped catch a murderer.

"Hey, buddy," I said softly, reaching up to scratch his favorite spot at his withers. "Some day, huh?"

You could say that, Cooper replied while he continued to nap, not bothering to lift his head. *I thought we were just here for your first horse show, but apparently, we solve crimes now too.*

To be fair, Ripley chimed in from where he sat outside the stall, *this wasn't exactly in the show program.*

The announcer's voice crackled over the speakers, "Derby riders, your moment of glory awaits! And remember, it's not about the ribbons—it's about the experience. Or so they say. But let's be honest, winning this class has been on your vision boards for months!"

Cooper snorted. *Humans really do make things complicated. All this scheming, stressing, and vision boarding—when in the end, it's us horses carrying them through it. But hey, at least the good ones remember it's a team sport.*

Jennifer. A familiar voice came from behind me.

I turned to find Miranda's ghost standing there, her usual sharp expression softened into something almost gentle. Her form seemed less solid, more translucent than before, like she was preparing to leave.

I need to thank you, she said quietly. *You did it. I know I didn't make it easy on you, but you did it. I have to admit, I wouldn't have expected my champion for justice to be a timid, middle-aged amateur rider.*

Hey, give her some credit, Ripley huffed. *She caught your killer AND stayed on Cooper. That's what I call multitasking.*

A faint smile flickered across Miranda's face. *You're right. I was wrong about a lot of things, including you, Jennifer.* She paused, her form shimmering slightly.

I spent my whole life believing success in this sport was all about perfection—the perfect distance, the perfect position, the perfect round. And I thought I was protecting the integrity of the sport by demanding excellence from everyone. But you proved there's more to it than that. You protected the sport in your own way—by caring enough to uncover the truth, by trusting yourself even when you were scared, and by using gifts that could have left you ridiculed. And in that same way, you braved showing for the first time against children and with trainers like me judging your every move. Sometimes the bravest thing isn't about being perfect—it's about being willing to try, even with the odds stacked against you.

Well, she's definitely not perfect, I'll give you that, Cooper chimed in. *But she tries hard and gives good treats, so she's a winner in my book.*

Miranda's laugh was gentle. *Yes, exactly. Thank you, Jennifer. For everything.* Her form began to fade, growing more transparent by the second. She gave Cooper a final look. *And Cooper? Take good care of her. She's got potential —even though she still can't see a distance.*

Then, to my surprise, she winked—I suspected for the first time in her life... or rather, death.

Before I could reply, Miranda's form dissolved completely, leaving behind nothing but a faint shimmer in the air and the lingering echo of her laugh.

I stood there for a moment, processing her words. My "gifts"—the ones I'd spent so long trying to ignore, pretending they weren't real—yet without them, we might never have discovered the truth about Miranda's death.

Maybe these abilities weren't just an inconvenience to hide from the world. Maybe they were meant for something more.

Well, Ripley said with a characteristic head tilt, *I guess that's at least one trainer who won't be critiquing your position anymore.*

"Jen! JEN!" Amy's voice cut through my thoughts as she came running down the aisle, waving something in her hand. "You're not going to believe this!"

Ten treats say you placed, Cooper muttered, nudging my shoulder.

Amy skidded to a stop in front of us, her face flushed with excitement. "You got a fourth in your third round! That's so good for your first show!"

She thrust the yellow, fourth-place ribbon at me. I took it slowly, running my fingers over the smooth satin.

I stared at it, dumbfounded. "But... my first round was awful."

"Oh, it was not! Don't be so hard on yourself. But either way, you came back and got better each time and nailed the last one! And that's what really counts—not giving up when things get hard. You should be so proud of yourself!" Amy squealed, her eyes bright. "I can't believe everything that's happened today. Between your first show and all the drama with Victoria... It's been intense but amazing! I hope you had fun!"

She grinned. "Oh! We need to get your sixth-place ribbon too so we can take a picture with Cooper."

I glanced down at the yellow ribbon. I already knew this wasn't what it was all about, and after everything that had happened today, I most definitely knew it never should be.

But standing here now, sore and exhausted, with this fifty-cent token of the day's efforts, I couldn't shake the feeling that I'd proven something—to myself if no one else.

What a day.

It certainly has been a day, Cooper said, his eyes still half-closed, his voice warm. *And for someone who was terrified to even enter the show ring this morning, you've done pretty well. I'm proud of ya, kid. Though, I expect you'll be back to overthinking your jumping position by Tuesday. As you probably should.*

I gave him a playful slap on the shoulder.

~

"Has anyone seen my show coat?" I called out, scanning our rapidly emptying tack area. Every muscle ached, and my brain felt like it was operating through fog. After the day's events—both in and out of the ring—I could barely remember what I was supposed to be doing.

"Check behind that pile of saddle pads. I think I saw it there," Amy suggested as she gathered up bridles. "Though you might want to look for your helmet first you asked about that five minutes ago."

"Oh. Right." End-of-show brain was real.

Cooper watched our pack-up efforts from his stall while he munched contentedly on hay. *You all are taking forever. Home is calling.*

"That derby was incredible," Amy said as she headed out of the tack room. "Rachel and Apollo were amazing. I can't believe they still pulled off that win after everything that happened."

"Thank God you caught Victoria when you did," Liz added, gathering water buckets. "The timing worked out perfectly—whatever she gave him earlier had worn off by derby time." She shook her head. "Miranda always said she'd do anything to protect the integrity of this sport. Guess she meant it."

Speaking of catching killers, Ripley chimed in from his supervisory position, *I think I deserve extra treats for my detective work today. That scent was unmistakable!*

Yes, yes, you're very clever, Cooper replied. *Though notice I'M the one who had to stay focused through both murder investigations AND hunter courses. Not exactly what they trained me for as a schoolmaster.*

"I know you didn't know her at all, but Miranda would have been proud of you," Amy said quietly. "Not just about finding out who killed her, but stopping Victoria before she could get to Apollo again. She was a tough trainer, but she loved the horses."

Little did she know how well I knew that.

I found my show coat right where Amy said it was and reached into the pocket to see if I had any peppermints left for Cooper. Instead, I found Detective Hayes's card. My fingers traced the embossed letters on the card.

I paused.

A few years ago, the most exciting thing in my pockets

had been grocery lists. Now I had a detective's card and horse treats. Mark would never believe it.

Maybe solving mysteries wasn't so different from learning to ride—both required determination, persistence, and the courage to do what it took. And maybe a little bit of crazy, as horse girls are known to be.

I smiled to myself—a horse girl. My childhood self practically squealed with glee.

And then there was the whole seeing ghosts and talking to animals bit... yeah, I was all kinds of crazy.

But now that didn't seem so bad.

The announcer's voice crackled over the speaker one final time. "And that's a wrap, folks! Some wins come with ribbons, some come with great stories, but at the end of the day, it's how you treat your horse that really matters."

He's not wrong, Cooper said. *Though next time, let's just have a regular horse show... hmmm? Maybe then you'll let me go to the jumps properly.*

I smiled, patting his neck. The barn had become so much more than just an escape—it had become the place where I rediscovered myself.

You're getting philosophical again, Ripley observed, stretching lazily. *Though I suppose catching murderers and earning your first ribbons in one day does that to a person.*

Cooper swung his head around to look at me. *Just remember what I said about doing the jumps properly next time. Fourth and sixth aren't bad for your first show, but you know I'm a schoolmaster, right? Imagine what we could do if you weren't distracted by crime-solving.*

I laughed, scratching his favorite spot. *Next time we'll focus purely on riding. Promise.*

As I helped Amy and Liz load the last of our equipment into the trailer, I couldn't help but smile. A couple of years ago, I'd thought I was too old for new beginnings. Instead, I'd found not just a new hobby, but a whole new life with barn friends, horse shows, and even my own oddball crime-solving crew.

Mark had always said I lived in a fantasy world. Turns out, he had no idea how right he was.

Come on, Cooper nickered softly. *Time to go home.*

Home. Now there was a word that meant something completely different than it had just a few months ago. And whatever adventures came next, I knew I had the perfect team to face them with.

Thank You for Reading!

Thank you for reading *Murder at the Horse Show*! I hope you enjoyed following Jen, Ripley, and Cooper on their first adventure. Keep a look out for more in the series!

If you have a moment, I'd truly appreciate it if you left a review. It helps other readers find the book and means the world to independent authors like me. Thank you!

About the Author

Like Jen, I was *not* one of those lucky kids who grew up riding ponies. I finally got my chance to dive into the horse world as a (ahem) mature adult, and I've been making up for lost time ever since! It's been exciting, humbling, and occasionally a little embarrassing, but I wouldn't trade it for anything.

These days, I'm lucky enough to have a horse of my own, Scotty, who keeps me on my toes in all the best ways.

Also like Jen, I have a Boston Terrier named Ripley. He's either zooming around the house, begging to play fetch, or passed out, snoring like a tiny freight train, though the cutest freight train you've ever seen!

We live on the west coast of Canada, with my ever-supportive, albeit somewhat reluctant, beta-reader husband.

Thanks so much for reading. I hope you join Jen, Ripley, and Cooper on their next adventure!

44627750R00062